THE ITALIAN'S CINDERELLA

LUCY GORDON

First published in Great Britain 2008
Harlequin Mills & Boon Limited,
Eton House, 18-24 Paradise Road, Richmond, Surrey TW9 1SR

ISBN: 978 0 263 86519 6

Set in Times Roman 13 on 14¾ pt
02-0608-49799

Printed and bound in Spain
by Litografia Rosés, S.A., Barcelona

Lucy Gordon cut her writing teeth on magazine journalism, interviewing many of the world's most interesting men, including Warren Beatty, Richard Chamberlain, Roger Moore, Sir Alec Guinness and Sir John Gielgud. She also camped out with lions in Africa, and had many other unusual experiences which have often provided the background for her books. She is married to a Venetian, whom she met while on holiday in Venice. They got engaged within two days. Two of her books have won the Romance Writers of America RITA® award, SONG OF THE LORELEI in 1990, and HIS BROTHER'S CHILD in 1998, in the Best Traditional Romance category.

You can visit her website at www.lucy-gordon.com

Dear Reader

I love the chance to write about Venice. It is like no other place in the world, with its freedom from cars, its mysterious silences, its sudden dangers, and above all its unique atmosphere of romance.

I know about that atmosphere, having myself fallen under its spell. Some years ago I took a holiday there, met a Venetian, became engaged to him in two days, and am now Venetian by marriage. So the Grand Canal and the Rialto Bridge have a special meaning for me, but it is the little places that mean even more—the tiny bridges, the narrow canals with washing strung across them, the backstreets where a couple can lose themselves, hopefully for ever.

This is what I have tried to celebrate in my story of Pietro and Ruth, two lost souls who find each other with the help of a magical city.

Warm wishes

Lucy Gordon

CHAPTER ONE

WHEN lightning filled the room, Pietro went to the window and looked out into the night.

He enjoyed a storm, especially when it swept over his beloved Venice, flashing down the Grand Canal, making the historic buildings tremble. To those who sighed over the beauties of Venice he would say that 'his' city was not the gentle, romantic site of legend, but rather a place of savage cruelty, treachery and murder.

Thunder crashed, engulfing him and the whole Palazzo Bagnelli, then dying, so that the only sound was the pounding of the rain on the water.

In the dim light he could just make out the Rialto Bridge looming up to his right, its shuttered windows glaring like blind eyes.

From beside him came a soft whine, and he reached out to scratch the head of a large, mongrel dog.

'It's all right, Toni,' he said. 'It's only noise.'

But he kept his hand on the rough fur, knowing that his friend had an affliction that made him nervous, and Toni moved closer.

Now it was dark again and he could see his own reflection in the glass. It was like looking at a ghost, which was apt, considering how ghostly his life was.

Even the building around him seemed insubstantial, despite its three floors of heavy stone. The Palazzo Bagnelli, home of the Counts Bagnelli for six centuries, was one of the finest buildings of its kind in Venice.

For many years its great rooms had been filled with notable personages; servants by the hundred had scurried along its passages. Lords and ladies in gorgeous clothes had paraded in its stately rooms.

Now they were all gone, leaving behind one man, Count Pietro Bagnelli, with neither wife nor child, nor any other close family. Only two servants were left, and he was content with that.

These days he invited nobody to his home, living a solitary life in a few rooms in a corner of the building, with only Toni for company. Even to himself it had a sense of unreality, especially in winter. It was only nine o'clock but darkness had fallen and the storm had driven everyone inside.

He moved away from the window towards another one at the corner, through which he could see both the Grand Canal and the narrow alley that ran alongside the palazzo.

The spectre in the glass moved with him, showing a tall man with a lean, face, mobile mouth and deep set eyes. It was a wry, defensive face, the eyes seeming to look out from a trapped place. He was thirty-four but his air of cautious withdrawal made him seem older.

Beside him Toni suddenly became agitated. He was big enough for his head to reach the window, and he'd seen something outside that made him scrabble to get closer and demand his master's attention.

'There's nothing out there,' Pietro told him. 'You're imagining things. *Dio mio!*'

The exclamation had been torn from him by a flash of lightning, even more blinding than the last, that had turned everything white. By its light he thought he'd seen a figure standing below in the alley.

'Now I'm imagining things as well,' he muttered. 'I must stop this.'

But he stayed there, trying to see through the darkness, and at last the lightning came again, flashing on and off, showing him the figure of a young woman, drenched, her hair plastered to her head, water streaming off her. Then the night swallowed her up again.

Frowning, he opened the window and looked out into the alley, half convinced that she was an illusion. But suddenly the moon came out from behind the clouds and he saw her again.

She was perfectly still, gazing up at the window, apparently oblivious to her surroundings.

He leaned out, calling, *'Ciao!'*

She neither moved nor spoke.

'Ciao!' he called again. Still in Italian he yelled, 'Wait, I'm coming down.'

He hated being disturbed but he couldn't leave her to freeze. In a moment he was heading down the stairs to the side entrance, wrenching open the heavy door.

Pietro had expected her to hurry inside, but she was still standing where he'd left her, so he hauled her forcibly inside, not troubling to be gentle. He would rescue her but he was damned if he was going to get soaked for her.

Holding her suitcase in one hand and her arm in the other, he hurried her up the stairs to his rooms, where she collapsed on the sofa, her eyes closing as she lost consciousness.

'Mio dio!' he muttered again, seeing the dilemma he was in.

He must get her into dry clothes fast, but the thought of undressing her while she was unconscious appalled him. Yet he couldn't let her get pneumonia. His housekeeper was away for the night. What he had to do must be done alone.

Hurrying into the bathroom, he seized a clean robe and a large towel. Her coat was light and soaked right through. Taking it off was easy, but then he knew he must remove her dress. He worked fast, praying that she might not awake until he was finished. To his relief she stayed dead to the world.

When she was decently swathed in the towel robe he rubbed her hair until it was no more than damp, then got some blankets, laid her on the sofa and placed them over her.

What the devil had happened to her? How had she ended up alone at night, in a thunderstorm, naked in the hands of a stranger? He'd tried not to notice details of her body, but he'd sensed that she was too thin, like someone who'd lost a lot of weight quickly.

'Wake up,' he pleaded.

When she didn't move he became desperate. Taking a glass and a decanter from the cupboard, he poured a measure of brandy, hauled her up and forced it to her lips. Some was spilt, but enough went down to make her sneeze and open her eyes.

'Good,' he said. 'Now finish drinking this.'

He gave her no choice, holding the glass to her lips until she'd drained it.

'Who are you?' Pietro asked in Italian. 'How do you come to be here?'

'Excuse me,' she whispered in English.

He too switched to English to say, 'Never mind. You need food and rest.'

But there was more here than simply malnutrition and weariness. She looked like someone on the edge of sanity, and he was sure of it when she began to murmur words that made no sense.

'I shouldn't have come—I knew it was a mistake, but there was nothing else to do—he's the only one who can tell me—but maybe it doesn't matter—only I have to know. I can't bear it any longer, not knowing.'

'Signorina—'

'Do you know what that's like? To wonder and wonder when there's nobody who can help you—and you think you may spend all your life in the shadows?'

Without his realising, his hands tensed on her shoulders.

'Yes,' he breathed. 'I know what that's like.'

'It doesn't end, does it?'

'No,' he said gravely, 'it doesn't end.'

Pietro closed his eyes, feeling the waves of suffering engulf him again. He'd thought he'd learned to cope, but she brought it back because she was abandoned in the same desert. He could sense her there, her gaze fixed on him, one lost soul reaching out to another.

'What can you do about it?' she asked.

'I don't know,' he said. 'I've never known.'

The look she turned on him was terrible, containing a despairing acceptance of something too sad for words.

'How did you get here?' he urged.

She looked around. 'Here?'

'You're in Venice. I found you standing in the street outside, just looking up.'

'I don't remember.'

'Never mind, tell me later.'

He returned from the kitchen after a few minutes to find her looking down at her strange attire with dismay.

'I had to take your clothes off,' he said quickly. 'You were sodden. But I swear I didn't—well—you know—'

To his total astonishment, she smiled.

'I know,' she said.

'You do believe me?'

'Yes, I believe you. Thank you.'

'Come and sit down at the table.'

As she came out of the shadows into the light he had a feeling that there was something familiar about her, but he couldn't place it. He must be mistaken. He wouldn't have forgotten this girl.

He ushered her to a chair, drawing it out for her and saying, 'When did you last eat?'

'I'm not sure. I missed breakfast because I was late, and had to dash. I was too nervous to eat at the airport, or on the plane. The storm was just getting really bad as we landed. I got so scared that I sat in the airport for an hour.'

'Don't you have a hotel? I know it can be hard to find one at this time of year. A lot of them close.'

'Oh, no, I came straight here.'

'To the Palazzo Bagnelli? Why?'

'I thought Gino might be here.'

'Gino Falzi?'

She brightened. 'You do know him?'

'Yes, I know him well, but—'

'Does he still live here? Is he here now?'

'No,' he said slowly.

Pietro was getting warning signals that filled him with apprehension.

Gino's mother had once been the Bagnelli family's cook, living on the premises with her son. The lads had grown up good friends despite the six years between them. Gino was light-hearted, delightful company, and Pietro, the elder and more serious-minded, had found in him a much-needed release.

'You should laugh more,' Gino often chided him. 'Come on, have some fun.'

And Pietro had laughed, following his scapegrace friend into his latest mad adventure, from which he usually had to extract him. Gino had a butterfly mind, which made it hard for him to settle to steady employment, although he had finally found a niche in the tourist firm that Pietro owned, where his charm made him a knockout with the customers.

It also made him a risk-taker, walking a fine line between acceptable behaviour and going a bit too far. Pietro knew that Gino loved to impress the girls by pretending that he came from the aristocratic Bagnelli family, and although he disapproved it also made him shrug wryly. It was just Gino amusing himself.

Now he was beginning to worry that Gino had amused himself in a way that might bring tragedy.

'Can you tell me where he is?' she asked.

'He's off travelling at the moment. He works for me in a tourist firm I own, and he's exploring new places.'

'But he'll be home soon?' she asked with a hint of eagerness that both touched and worried him.

'No, he's on a long trip, finding places where I can mount tours.'

'I see,' she said with a little sigh.

Pietro asked his next question carefully.

'Does Gino know you well?'

At first he thought she hadn't heard, so long did she take to reply. Then she shook her head.

'No,' she said. 'He won't know me. Nobody knows me any more. I don't know myself, or anybody else. I know who I was then—'

'Then?' he queried gently. 'When was that?'

'About a year ago—or perhaps a little more. I've got the date written down somewhere—' She saw his troubled face and gave a half smile that was oddly charming. 'I sound quite mad, don't I?'

'I don't think you're mad at all,' he said firmly.

'You could be wrong about that. I've been in a special home for—well, most of the last year. Now I'm trying to find my way back into the world, only I don't do it very well.'

'Then it's lucky you found a safe place, and a friend,' he said.

'How can you be my friend when you don't know who I am? Whoever I was then, I'm someone else now. I just don't know who.'

'You must know your name or how could you travel?'

'My name is Ruth Denver.'

A spoon fell out of Pietro's hand and hit the terrazzo floor with a ping. Cursing his own clumsiness, he leaned down to pick it up, glad of the chance to hide his face, lest it reveal his shock at hearing the name Ruth Denver.

When he looked up again he was in control and able to say calmly, 'My name is Pietro Bagnelli.'

'Gino's cousin?' she exclaimed, her eyes suddenly glowing. 'He told me a lot about you, how you grew up together.'

'We'll talk some more in the morning,' he interrupted her hastily. 'You'll be better when you've slept.'

He was becoming more disturbed every moment, and needed to be alone to do some thinking before he talked further. If she was who he was beginning to believe she was, he needed to tread with care.

'I'll get a room ready for you,' he said. Pausing at the door, he added, 'Don't go away.'

She regarded him quizzically, and he realised he sounded crazy. Where could she go? But he had a strange feeling that if he took his eyes off her she might vanish into thin air.

'I promise not to disappear,' she said with a glimmer of humour that was evident even through her distress.

'Just to make sure you don't—Toni, on guard.'

The huge mutt came forward and laid his head on Ruth's knee.

'Stay like that, both of you, until I get back,' Pietro said.

In the next room there was a couch that could be turned into a bed. He made it up, his mind in turmoil. What was happening was impossible. There was no way that this could be Ruth Denver.

He returned to the living room to find that both its occupants had obeyed him. Toni's head was still on Ruth's knee, and she was stroking it, regarding the dog with a smile of fond indulgence.

'Your room's ready,' he said. 'Try to get plenty of sleep. I won't let anything disturb you.'

'Thank you,' she said softly, and slipped away.

As soon as he was alone Pietro poured himself a large brandy. He had never needed one so much.

He felt stunned.

At first he'd thought this might be one of Gino's discarded girlfriends who hadn't given up hope. It happened often, but there were reasons why it couldn't be the answer this time.

As Pietro brooded on those reasons he grew more and more troubled.

Just over a year ago Gino had fallen in love with an English girl, a tourist in Venice. Pietro had been away at the time and when he returned she'd gone back to England, so he'd never met her.

For once Gino had seemed genuinely smitten, to the point of marriage. Pietro's wedding gift was going to be a grand reception in the palazzo.

'But I want to meet this paragon,' he told his

young friend. 'She must be really special to persuade you to settle down.'

'Yes, she really is special,' Gino enthused. 'You'll love her.'

'I hope not,' Pietro teased. 'I'm a respectable married man.'

'And you don't want Lisetta throwing pots and pans at you.'

'She never would,' Pietro said quietly. 'She thinks of nothing but pleasing me.'

'So I should hope. And imagine how pleased you're going to be when she gives birth to that son. When is it due now?'

'One month.'

'We'll have the wedding just after that.'

It was arranged that Gino would go to England for the firm, and bring his fiancée back with him for a pre-wedding visit. His work in England had been expected to last two weeks, but he was home in five days, mysteriously pale and quiet, which was so unlike Gino as to be alarming. In response to Pietro's concerned questions he would only say that the marriage was off. He and his lover would never meet again.

As far as Pietro could tell Gino never called her, and if his cell phone rang he jumped. But it was never her.

'Did you quarrel?' Pietro asked cautiously. 'Did she catch you flirting?'

'Not at all. She just changed her mind.'

'She dumped *you?'* Pietro asked, incredulous. Such a thing had never happened before.

'That's right, she dumped me, and asked me to leave her alone.'

Before Pietro could explore further, his wife went into premature labour, and died giving birth to a son, who also died. In the aftermath of that tragedy all thoughts of Gino's problems were driven from his mind.

When he was able to function again he saw that his friend hadn't recovered his spirits. Pietro's kind heart prompted him to send Gino away on a number of trips, seeking out new destinations for the firm.

Now and then Gino returned to Venice, seeming more cheerful. But always his first question was whether there had been any news from England, and Pietro realised that this young woman had callously broken his heart.

Her name had been Ruth Denver.

'But it can't be her,' he growled to himself. 'She doesn't look anything like her. I've seen her picture—'

In a cupboard he found a book full of photographs and went through them until he found the one he wanted. It showed Gino just over a year ago, handsome, laughing, his arm around a young girl. She too was laughing, her face full of joy as she gazed at him. Peering closer, Pietro managed to recognise her as Ruth Denver. But only just.

This was a big, buxom girl, generously made, with a broad, confident smile. Her hair was thick and long, flowing over her shoulders, somehow hinting at an equally expansive nature.

The ethereal creature who had invaded his home tonight was a ghost of her former self. Her hair was short, almost boyish, her smile had died, her eyes were sad and cautious. Small wonder he hadn't recognised her at first.

What had happened to change her from one person into the other?

When she was exhausted the impressions swirled about her head and ran together. She was asleep, yet not asleep, her dreams haunted by a man who came out of nowhere, seized her and took her to safety. In the darkness and rain she couldn't make out his face. Only his strength and determination were real.

Then the rain vanished and she was lying on a sofa while he pressed a brandy on her, forceful yet gentle, both together. She didn't know who he was yet every detail was mysteriously clear. She could see his face now, handsome but for a tautness about the mouth, giving him a withered look that shouldn't have been there for several years.

When he rose and moved about the room there was grace in his movements, except that he seemed always ready against an attack. Or perhaps the attack would come from him, for she sensed something below the surface that might explode at any moment, all the more dangerous for the quietness of his voice.

Then the impressions shifted, whirled away into the darkness, replaced by another time, another place. Now she was smiling as she was swept back to the time of happiness.

There was Gino, gazing at her, giving her the fond smile she adored, reaching for her hand across the restaurant table, caressing her fingers with his lips.

'They're staring at us,' she whispered, looking around at the other diners.

'So let them,' he said merrily. 'Oh you English, you're so cold.'

'Me? Cold?'

'No, never, *carissima.* You're a dream of perfection, and I love you madly.'

'Say it in Venetian,' she begged. 'You know I love that.'

'Te voja ben—te voja ben—'

How could there be such joy in the world? Her handsome Gino had come to England to take her back to Venice where his family were waiting to welcome her. Soon they would be married, living together in that lovely city.

'I love you too,' she said. 'Oh, Gino, we're going to be so happy.'

But without warning the darkness came down, obscuring first his face, then everything. Suddenly the world was full of pain. He was gone.

There were flickers—more pictures, but they came from much earlier. There was Gino as he'd been on the day they met in Venice, winning her heart with his cheeky humour and glowing admiration. She'd been struggling with the language, and he'd come to her aid. Somehow they had ended up spending the evening together, and he'd made her talk about herself.

'You know so many languages,' he'd said, 'French, German, Spanish, but no Italian. That's very bad. You should learn Italian without delay.'

'But do I really need another language?' she'd asked, not because she really objected, but to provoke an answer.

There had been a special significance in his look as he'd said, 'Well, I'm glad you couldn't speak it today, or we wouldn't have met. But now I really think you should learn.'

After that he had set himself to teach her his language, and done it very thoroughly.

More pictures—the airport where he'd seen her off, almost in tears from the strength of his feelings. Then the call to say he was coming to England, the ecstatic meeting, and that last evening together—

'You're a dream of perfection, and I love you madly—*te voja ben—te voja ben—*'

'Te voja ben,' she whispered longingly.

There was his face as he said it, but it was fading, fading—

'Gino!'

She screamed again and again, stretching out her arms in a frantic attempt to hold on to him.

'Come back,' she cried. 'Come back. Don't leave me.'

But then she touched him. She couldn't see him but she could feel that he'd turned back to her, was taking her in his arms, drawing her against his body.

'Where did you go?' she sobbed. 'I was so scared—I longed for you—where were you?'

Strong arms tightened about her, and she heard the soothing words murmured in her ear.

'It's all right, don't panic. I'm here.'

'Don't leave me again.'

'I won't leave you as long as you need me.'

'Where have you been?' she whispered. 'I've missed you so much.'

She reached for his face and kissed it again and again in her passionate relief, his forehead, his cheeks, his mouth. To her surprise he didn't kiss her back, but at least he was there.

'Te voja ben,' she whispered. *'Te voja ben.'*

'Lie back,' he said, gently pushing her down against the pillow. 'You're safe now.'

She could still feel his hands clasping hers, and their strength calmed her. Her terror began to fade. After so long among nightmares and mystery, Gino had finally returned, his arms open to her.

'Sleep now,' he whispered. 'And in the morning everything will be all right.'

But something perverse in her, something awkward that months of misfortune hadn't managed to stifle, made her open her eyes.

A man was sitting on her bed, holding her hands. Even in the semi-darkness she could tell that it wasn't Gino.

CHAPTER TWO

PIETRO was in pyjamas and his hair was tousled. He switched on the small bedside light and watched as the joy died out of her eyes.

'I heard you calling,' he said. 'You sounded desperate.'

'I had such dreams,' she whispered. 'Gino—'

He wondered if she knew that she'd kissed him, thinking he was Gino, and cried out; '*Te voja ben,*' the Venetian for 'I love you.' With all his soul he hoped not.

'Talk to me about Gino,' he said.

'Our last evening together—I have that dream so often, but then it fades—he vanishes, but I don't know where—and it's too late to find out because it was so long ago. I'm sorry if I awoke you. I promise to be quiet now.'

'You can't help a dream.'

She suddenly put her hands together over her chest, but there was nothing seductive about her appearance. Like him, she was in pyjamas. They were sedate and functional, buttoning high in the front.

'I didn't mean to stare at you,' he assured her.

'Don't worry,' she said simply. 'I'm used to it.'

'I don't understand.'

'I warned you last night that I was a bit mad.'

'Don't talk like that,' he said quickly.

'Why not? It's true—well, a little bit. For the last year I've been officially diagnosed as "disturbed". I'm a lot better than I was, but I'm not all the way there yet.'

'But what happened? Can you tell me?'

'Gino came to England. We went out to dinner and—' She stopped, smiling. 'We talked about how I was going back to Venice with him, to meet his family, and discuss the wedding. It was the most marvellous night of my life, until—until—'

'Don't force yourself if it's too painful.'

'I have to, or I'll never escape.'

'All right,' he said quietly. 'Tell me what happened.'

At last Ruth began to speak.

'When we'd finished eating we went out to the car park, and found some lads there, trying to break into the car. They attacked us. I was knocked out, and woke up in the hospital. My mind was a blank. I didn't know what had happened, or who I was. I didn't even recognise Gino.

I only knew there was a young man sitting beside the bed, but to me he was a stranger. Everything in my mind was blank, including myself.

'But seeing him again afterwards, didn't that help you to remember?'

'I don't remembering him coming back—but he may have done. I kept blacking out. When I awoke properly it was some time later and he wasn't there. I never saw him again. Perhaps he couldn't bear my not recognising him any longer. I can't blame him for leaving.'

Pietro was getting a very bad feeling about this. Gino's story that he'd been jilted had always sounded unlikely. In truth, he seemed to have deserted her when she most needed him.

'And you had nobody to help you? No family? Nothing?'

'After my parents died I was raised by my mother's sister, who didn't really want me. She died while I was away at college. Then I discovered that she'd known for months that she was dying, but never told me. It was like the final slamming of a door.

'So there was nobody who'd known me in the past. I had blinding headaches. There was a lot of pressure on my brain because I'd been beaten so badly about the head. They had to operate to relieve it. I was better after that.'

'But—alone,' he murmured, stunned by the horror of it.

She gave a little wry smile.

'I looked awful. I was rather glad there was nobody to see me.'

Pietro was speechless. Perhaps, he thought, it was a good thing Gino wasn't present right now. He might have said or done something he would later regret.

'All my hair was shaved off,' she recalled. 'I looked like a malignant elf.'

Something in her self-mocking tone inspired him to say absurdly, 'Why malignant? I always thought elves were nice.'

'Not this one. I even scared myself. My memory started to return in bits. It was odd, I'm a language teacher and I found I still knew the languages, but not my own identity.

'I was able to get some official records, and the people I knew at work could tell me a few things that I'd told them about myself. But effectively my life started when I awoke in the hospital.'

'How long were you there?' he asked.

'Three or four months. Then I was moved into sheltered accommodation. I was too full of nerves to go back to teaching in a school, but I managed to get some translation work to do at home. That made me feel better, and my mind seemed to open up a little more every day.

'At last I remembered who I was, and Gino—how much we loved each other—it all came back in a rush, while I was asleep. I went back to the hospital to see if anyone there could remember seeing him, but of course it was in the past, and most of the staff had changed.

'So in the end I decided to come back to Venice. I hoped to find him but if—if not, I can go back to the places where we were together, and see if anything more comes back to me.'

'What are you hoping for?' he asked. 'That you'll rediscover your love?'

'I'm not really sure. But there are so many gaps that only he can fill in. I can't even remember much of the attack. The lads were never caught. It was a year ago, but to me it was yesterday.'

Which means that it was yesterday she'd sat in the restaurant with Gino, exchanging words of love. Part of her, at least, was still in love with him. Pietro was sick at heart.

'I suppose he might be married by now,' she said softly. 'I can't hope that he still loves me just because I—' She broke off.

'No, he isn't married,' Pietro said heavily.

'But for him it's been a long time. I know.' She suddenly gave him a delightful smile. 'Don't worry. I haven't come to make trouble. I just want him to help me move forward.'

Ruth seemed to become self-conscious. 'Perhaps you should go away now. I don't want to make trouble for you either—I mean your wife. Gino told me about her, and the baby you were expecting. I hope I haven't disturbed either of them.'

'No, you haven't disturbed them,' Pietro said abruptly. 'They're both dead. Goodnight.'

He left quickly.

Back in his own room he tried to sleep, but now it was impossible. The trouble with letting a ghost into his home was that she had brought other ghosts with her. He spent his life trying to avoid those gentle phantoms, and now they were here, making him feel their sadness.

Not that Lisetta had ever reproached him. She'd loved him too well for that. More than life, she'd often said. And proved it. And the baby, dead after only a few hours, now sleeping peacefully in his mother's arms, a reminder of what might have been.

'Go away,' he cried desperately. 'Haven't I been punished enough?'

It was an hour before he fell into an exhausted sleep, and when he awoke it was broad daylight, and he could hear Minna, his housekeeper, moving about outside. He wondered if the two women had met. But when he went out there was only Minna, large, middle-aged, the epitome of solid reassurance.

'About that lady,' he said when they had greeted each other.

'What lady, signore?'

'Haven't you seen her? She stayed the night here because of the storm. Perhaps she's still in her room.'

But the room was empty. The bed had been stripped and the bedclothes folded neatly. Ruth's suitcase was gone.

'There's a letter for you on the table,' Minna said.

With a sense of foreboding he snatched it up and found his worst fears realised.

'I'm really sorry to have bothered you,' it said. 'I had no idea about your wife. Please forgive me. Thank you for all you did. Ruth.'

'Stupid woman!' he growled, crushing the letter.

'Signore?'

'Not you, Minna. Her. What does she think she's playing at? You didn't catch a glimpse of her leaving?'

'No, signore. There was nobody here when I came in. Just the letter on the table. What has this woman done?'

What had she done? he wondered. Only invaded his life, destroyed his peace, turned everything upside down, made him feel responsible for her welfare and then vanished into thin air. Nothing, really.

'I'm sorry, signore.'

'What for? It's not your fault. It's just that when I find her I'm going to strangle her.'

'Have some breakfast first.'

'No time. I don't know how long she's been gone.'

He vanished out of the door as he spoke, hurrying down the narrow *calle* that ran alongside the palazzo. It ended in a small square where there were a few shops, at one of which a man was arranging groceries outside.

'Enrico, have you seen a young woman come out of here?' Pietro described her.

'Yes, about an hour ago. She went down that turning.'

'Thank you,' he called over his shoulder.

Luck was with him. It was January and Venice was almost free of tourists, plus, in that tiny city, he knew almost every other resident, so he was able to consult many kindly friends, and managed to build up a picture of Ruth's movements, even down to half an hour she spent drinking coffee in a small café.

In no other city but Venice could he have done this. The word began to spread ahead of him. People telephoned each other to ask if Ruth had passed that way, then they began waiting for him in the squares and alleyways, and one was even able to describe the new coat she'd just bought. It was dark red wool, very stylish, he assured Pietro, and a great improvement on the light coat she'd been wearing, which was damp.

It was a help. Now he was able to look for the coat, and finally he spotted her in the Garibaldi Gardens, at the extreme end of Venice, where the land tailed off into the lagoon.

He almost didn't see her at first. By now, it was late afternoon, the light was fading fast and she was sitting quite still on a stone bench. Her elbows were resting on her knees and her arms were crossed as if to protect herself, but she didn't, as he'd feared, have the look of despair he'd seen last night. She merely seemed calm and collected.

After the frazzled day he'd had, the sight had an unfortunate effect on his temper. He planted himself in front of her.

'I've spent all day looking for you,' were his first cross words.

'But didn't you get my letter?'

'Yes, I got it, for what good you thought it did. The state you were in— Just running off— Of all the daft—' He exploded into a stream of Venetian curses while she waited for him to be finished.

'But can't you see that I had to do it?' Ruth asked when she could get a word in.

'No, I can't,' he snapped.

'I just felt so embarrassed about dumping myself on you like that.'

'You didn't. I hauled you in. That was my first mistake.'

'You wish you'd left me there?'

'I wish I'd chucked you in the Grand Canal. But I didn't. I invited you into my home, where you collapsed.'

'But if I'd known about your wife—'

'Why should you? Leave that.'

There was a silence, then she said awkwardly, 'And now you're angry with me.'

Remembering her frail condition, he knew he should utter comforting words, designed to make her feel better. But something had got hold of him and the words poured out in a stream of ill temper.

'Why should you think that? I only dashed out without any breakfast and spent the day wandering the streets looking for the most awkward, difficult woman I've ever met. I'm tired, I'm hungry, I'm cold, and it was all completely unnecessary. Why the devil should I be angry with you?'

Instead of bursting into tears she regarded him thoughtfully before saying, 'I expect you feel a lot better now you've lost your temper.'

'Yes!'

It was true. All his life he'd been even-tempered. That had changed in the last year, when rage would sometimes overcome him without warning, but he'd put his mind to controlling these outbursts, and succeeded up to a point. But these days self-control had a heavy price, and now the relief of allowing himself an explosion was considerable.

'Can I buy you a drink?' she asked.

'You can buy me two,' he growled. 'Come on, let's go, it's getting dark.'

Pietro grasped her hand firmly, so as not to lose her again, and reached for her suitcase. But she tried to hold on to it, protesting, 'I'm quite capable of—'

'Quit arguing and let go!'

He took her to a small café overlooking the lagoon, and they sat at the window, watching lights on the water. She bought him a large brandy, which he drained in one gulp, at which she ordered another.

'I'm sorry,' she said.

'So you ought to be. Of all the stupid, stupid—'

'OK, I get the point. I'm stupid.'

'Yes, *no!* I didn't mean it like that.' With horror he realised how his careless words might sound after what she'd been through. 'I don't want you to think—just because your head was injured—'

Then he saw that she was giving him a quizzical half-smile.

'It's all right,' she said kindly. 'You don't have to tread on eggshells. Let's leave it that I'm crazy but I'm not stupid.'

'Stop that talk! You're not crazy.'

'How do you know?' she demanded indignantly.

'Why are you suddenly different? Last night you were half out of it, and today you're ready to fight the world.'

'Isn't fighting better than giving in?'

'Sure, if you fight the right person. But why me?' he demanded, exasperated. 'Why am I getting all your aggro dumped on me?'

'You're handy.'

'That's what I thought.'

'I'd had a bad time yesterday, what with the flight and getting soaking wet. There's nothing like half drowning for making you depressed. But I've sorted myself out a bit now. Why are you glaring at me? What have I done wrong *now*?'

'All day I've had nightmares about you wandering Venice alone, confused, miserable. I was sorry for you, worried about you—and now you're fine.'

'Well, I'm sorry about that. Last night the pressure made me slip back to my bad time, but I've pulled myself together.'

He wasn't totally convinced. Her smile was too

bright, not quite covering an air of strain, and he guessed that part of this was presented for his benefit. But certainly she was mentally stronger than he had feared.

'I'm glad you're better,' he said, 'but you're still not ready to go wandering off among strangers. Whatever you may have thought, I didn't want you to go.'

'Of course you did—'

'Woman, what will it take to stop you arguing every time I open my mouth?'

'I don't know. If I think of something I'll make sure you never find out.'

'I'll bet you will.'

'I was just so embarrassed when I found out about your wife and child.'

'You needn't be,' he said, pale but speaking normally. 'They died nearly a year ago. I've come to terms with it by now.' Abruptly he changed the subject. 'I'm ready for something to eat, on me this time.'

She knew he wasn't telling the truth. He was far from coming to terms with his tragedy. His eyes spoke of a hundred sleepless night, and days that were even worse. He looked like a man who could be destroyed by his feelings, and, strangely, it made her feel calmer, as though in some mysterious way they were alike; equals in suffering, in need.

'As long as you know that I'm sorry,' she said slowly.

'You've nothing to feel bad about. You've even done me a favour, giving me something to think about apart from myself.'

'Oh, yes!' she said fervently.

He gave a faint smile. 'You too?'

'I'll say. After a while you get so bored with yourself.'

He ordered a meal, and while they waited he took out his cell phone and called Minna.

'It's all right, I've found her,' he said. 'If you'd just make up her bed—oh, you have. Thank you. Then I shan't need you again today. Have an early night.'

'That was my housekeeper,' he explained, shutting off the phone.

'And she's already made my bed up?'

'She never doubted that I'd bring you back.'

'Now I remember. Gino once said that none of your servants ever doubted that you could do everything you said you would. It's an article of faith, and practically heresy to doubt *il conte.*'

He made a wry face.

'It sounds devoted but actually it's just a way of controlling me.'

'I suppose people's expectations can be like handcuffs.'

'Exactly. It's one of the reasons I've always

tried to keep my head down and not be *il conte* any more than I have to. But it doesn't work. I've got the name hanging around my neck, and that great palace. How can any man live a normal life in a place like that?'

'It must be grim if you're there alone.'

'I'm not exactly alone. Minna lives there, and Celia, a maid. And Toni.'

'I love Toni,' she said at once. 'He's so big and shambling. I'm not sure why but he looks terribly vulnerable.'

'I got him from a rescue centre. Nobody else wanted him because he's epileptic, and I suppose they thought it might make him aggressive. It doesn't. Quite the reverse. When he has a fit he just lies there and shakes.'

'Poor soul,' she said, shocked. 'So you gave him a home because he had nowhere else to go.'

'Well, if I did he's repaid me a thousand times. He's the best friend a man ever had.'

But still, Ruth thought, shivering as she recalled that great empty building, it must make for a lonely life, with only his memories for company. She wondered about his wife, and how much he must have loved her to have been reduced to such bleakness by her loss. And she shivered again.

'Where did you go when you slipped out this morning?' Pietro asked.

'Looking for places I'd been before, but I didn't do so well. It's all so different in winter. I went to a little café where we'd been together. We sat outside, and I remember the sun shining on his hair, but today I stayed inside because it was drizzling. I can't do it on my own. I'll have to wait until he returns. Or maybe I could go to see him.'

'No,' he said quickly. 'It has to be here, where you were together.'

Pietro knew he must keep her with him at least until he'd spoken to Gino. Earlier that day he'd sat by the lagoon and put through a call on his cell phone. A female voice had answered. Pietro had left a message for Gino to call him, but nothing had happened.

He'd sent a text, stressing the urgency but not mentioning Ruth's name. Now, hours later, while Ruth was drinking her wine he did a hasty check under the table, but found nothing.

'How did you find me?' she asked.

'With the help of a few hundred friends. Venice counts as a great city because it's unique, but in size it's little more than a village. We all know each other. Sooner or later I found someone who'd seen you, and could point me in the right direction. I even knew what your new coat looked like.'

'So I've been under surveillance?'

'In a nice way. You can't hide anything from

your neighbours in Venice, but it can be comforting to have so many people look out for you.'

'Yes,' she said. 'Most of them said something about how I shouldn't be out so early in the cold, and I should be careful not to get lost.' She gave a sigh of pleasure. 'It was like being protected by a huge family.'

'We do that,' he agreed. 'Venetians are so different from the rest of the world. We try to look after the others.'

Except Gino, who had simply deserted her, he thought. He wondered if she were thinking the same, but she gave no sign.

'Go on telling me about your day,' he urged.

'Oh, you'd have laughed if you could have seen me. I had all sorts of impractical ideas, take a gondola ride, feed the pigeons in St Mark's Square, go to look at the Bridge of Sighs. Something really did come back to me there—the first time I got cross with him and we ended up bickering.'

'About the Bridge of Sighs?'

'Yes. Gino spun me the whole romantic story, how it had been named after the sighs of lovers. I thought that was lovely until I bought a guide book and discovered that the bridge connects the prison to the Doge's Palace, where trials were held. So the sighs came from prisoners taking their last look at the sky before going to the dungeons.'

Pietro began to laugh. 'You quarrelled about that?'

'Not quarrelled, squabbled. I like to have the truth.'

'Rather than a romantic fantasy? Shame on you.'

'I don't trust fantasies. They lay traps.'

'But so does the truth sometimes,' he pointed out quietly.

She didn't answer in words, but she nodded.

'I got very lofty and humourless,' she said after a while. 'I told Gino sternly that he had no right to tell lies just to make things sound romantic when they weren't. D'you know what he said?'

Pietro shook his head.

'He said, "But, *cara,* one of the prisoners was Casanova, the greatest lover in the history of the world. You can't get more romantic than that."'

He had to laugh at her droll manner. 'Did you forgive him?'

'Of course. You have to forgive Gino his funny little ways.'

He noted her use of the present tense, as though Gino were still a presence in her life. Was this how she explained his desertion to herself? Gino's funny little ways?

Ruth went on talking about her day, putting a light-hearted gloss on it, while he watched her with a heavy heart. A stranger would never have known the anguish that lay behind her flippant manner. But he saw it, because it was like looking at himself.

CHAPTER THREE

'THE trouble with you,' Pietro said at last, 'is that you're not organised. You need to do this properly, with someone who knows Venice and who can keep an eye on you to stop you doing something daft.'

'Well, I'm interviewing applicants for the position,' Ruth said promptly. 'There's no salary, unpredictable hours and it needs to be someone who can put up with me.'

'I'll consider myself hired.'

'I haven't offered you the job yet,' she protested in mock indignation.

'Fine. Shall I wait at the end of the queue? If you're wise you'll snap me up while I'm on offer.'

'Now which one of us is mad?' she chided him.

'Fifty-fifty, I'd say. It's best that way. We may be the only people in the world who can cope with each other.'

'But haven't you got your firm to run?'

'I have a good manager, and January isn't busy.'

They left the restaurant and wandered back to the path by the water just as a *vaporetto* approached the landing stage.

'That'll take us down the Grand Canal as far as we need to go,' Pietro said, seizing her hand and beginning to run.

They made it onto the great water-bus just in time, and laughed, holding themselves against the rails until a wave made the boat lurch, sending her stumbling against him. He steadied her, reminded again how insubstantial she was.

But then she gave him a cheerful smile and he realised that it was only her body that was frail. Tonight he'd glimpsed her cheeky fighting spirit, and he liked it.

'Shall we sit down for safety?' he asked.

'No, thanks, I'm fine.'

Ruth fixed one hand onto the upright rail and leaned slightly over the side, gazing down into the water rushing by. With a sigh of resignation Pietro wound an arm about her waist, holding her safe. It was simpler than remonstrating with her.

But it was a mistake, bringing back the previous night when she'd put her arms about his neck, kissing him again and again in the joy of eager young love. It had been so long since a woman had kissed him that he'd tensed, holding himself still, not responding to the shock, then waking her gently.

To his relief she hadn't seemed to know what had happened, and he'd managed to block it out of his mind. But it was there again now, her lips on his mouth, her body pressed against his, sweet and vulnerable. He tried to banish the memory, knowing that he had no right to it. It belonged to Gino, to a man who hadn't cared enough to claim it.

As soon as they got home he bid her goodnight and hurried to his own room to check his cell phone, but there was no message. Annoyed, he dialled, and, to his relief, Gino answered.

'Sorry, sorry, I know you said it was urgent,' came his cheery voice. 'But I'm a bit tied up.'

'Then get untied and talk to me about Ruth Denver.'

There was a silence.

'What about her?' Gino asked in a thin voice.

'She's here.'

'*What?* How?'

There was no mistaking the tone of his voice, Pietro thought grimly. Gino was aghast.

'She came to find you. She needs your help to recover from her injuries. Gino, you said she dumped you. You never mentioned an attack.'

'Look—it's not— The attack has nothing to do with it. She did dump me.'

'That's not what she says.'

'What—exactly does she say?'

Through the ultra-cautious words Pietro could sense the cogs and wheels of the lad's mind turning, and it filled him with dismay.

'She says you spent a loving evening together at the restaurant, then you were attacked by thugs. After that she lost her memory. When she saw you again she didn't recognise you.'

'Oh, she recognised me all right. We didn't have a loving evening. She told me it was over. I haunted the hospital until I knew she was better, but when she saw me she told me to go. Why do you think I never got in touch with her again? Because that was what she wanted.'

Pietro groaned, not knowing what to believe.

'What did she mean about me helping her with her injuries?' Gino asked.

'She has gaps in her memory and she wants you to help fill them.'

'That explains a lot. Pietro, this is one very troubled lady. She doesn't know what really happened and what didn't.'

'All the more reason for you to come back and help clear her mind.'

'But surely I'll just confuse her more? What's that?' Gino's voice sounded as though he'd turned his head to reply to someone. Then it became stronger again. 'Look, I've got to go. There's someone at the door.'

The line went dead.

Pietro cursed, knowing that Gino had made an excuse to escape.

He was more worried than he wanted to admit. It was just possible that Gino's version was correct, and Ruth was so disturbed that she didn't know what had really happened. She'd even partially admitted that.

But then he recalled her smiling as she said, 'You have to forgive Gino his funny little ways.'

There had been a kindly tolerance in her voice that simply didn't fit with the picture Gino was trying to paint. That was surely the real Ruth, forgiving and generous?

For some reason he wanted to believe this of her. But how could he tell when even she didn't know the full truth about herself? For the first time he fully understood the implications of her confusion, and how it might prove to be a nightmare, not only for her, but also perhaps for him.

Over breakfast next morning Pietro said, 'I have a few things to check, then I'm ready to take up my new position as your right-hand man.'

'Look, that was only a joke,' Ruth said hastily. 'I don't really expect you to give up your time to me.'

'You may have been joking. I wasn't. You should try to relax. The more you worry, the less clear your mind will become.'

The rain had gone and it was a fine morning as they set out to walk to St Mark's Piazza. Along the way the shops were opening, the owners arranging goods outside, smiling as they saw Pietro. Most of them hailed him, and some eyed Ruth with a look that said, 'Ah, you found her, then?'

She smiled back, relishing the feeling of being enveloped in kindness.

Through squares, along *calles* so narrow that she could touch both sides at once, and over tiny bridges, they finally reached the huge piazza. At one end was the glorious cathedral. On the other three sides were elegant arches, behind which were commercial establishments. One of these was Pietro's headquarters, a place where trips and hotels could be booked and various necessities hired.

'I'll introduce you to Mario,' Pietro said. 'He's a brilliant manager, although a little too meek for this violent city.'

'Violent?' Ruth queried. 'But surely it's a gentle, peaceful place. That's why they call it La Serenissima?'

'La Serenissima is only serene on the surface. Underneath it's another story, sometimes a cruel one.'

She had a partial demonstration as soon as they

entered, and she saw Mario, a young man with a plump, amiable face and an air of innocence. He was trying to cope with a middle-aged woman who was talking loudly and furiously.

'It's no excuse to say that they're booked up—'

'But, signora,' Mario pleaded, 'if that trip has no spaces left for that date, what can I do? Perhaps the next day—'

'I want that day!' she snapped.

Mario looked frazzled.

'Excuse me,' Pietro murmured.

In seconds he had the matter under control, convincing the lady politely but firmly that tantrums would get her nowhere. He even managed to persuade her to book for the following day. Mario watched, almost with tears in his eyes.

When the woman had gone, Pietro introduced the two of them.

'*Padrone,* I'm so sorry,' Mario started to say.

'Forget it,' Pietro said kindly. 'Nature just didn't design you to be a forceful man.'

'I'm afraid not,' Mario said, crestfallen.

'But in every other way you're an excellent manager, so let this matter go. How's business apart from ill-tempered ladies?'

'Doing well,' Mario hastened to tell him. 'There's hardly a hotel room left.'

'I thought everything was empty in January,' Ruth said.

'It's empty now, but in four weeks we start Carnival,' Pietro told her. 'And nobody wants to miss that. For eleven days the city will be packed. Everyone will eat too much, drink too much, and enjoy themselves in any way they please—also too much. But that's all right, they wear masks, so they get away with it.'

The rear of the shop was taken up with the hire department. There were printed catalogues, and large screens on which costumes could be projected.

But the real thing was also there, masks and outrageous costumes, all glowing with life and colour; brilliant reds and blues, vibrant greens and yellows, glittering with sequins and tinsel.

Mario, who had followed her while Pietro glanced through the books, began to show them off.

'These will be hired for the street parties,' he explained. 'For the big indoor occasions everyone will be much grander.'

He held one of the masks before his face. It was fierce and sexy in a slightly satanic way, and it transformed him into a man many women would find intriguing. Then he removed it and became gentle, sweet-natured Mario again.

'Ah, well,' he sighed. 'I can dream, can't I? That's what Carnival is for.'

'Perhaps your dream will come true,' she said, liking him.

'No, signorina. I dream of the lady who won't be disappointed when she sees the real me. If only I could keep this mask on for ever.'

'You might not like that as much as you think,' she mused. 'In the long run it's best to be yourself—whoever that is.'

'But to be a stranger, even to yourself, can be such a pleasure, especially when you can choose which stranger to be.'

'I suppose that's true,' she murmured, looking through some of the female masks. 'Being able to choose would make all the difference.'

She began to try them on, starting with one that was made like a cat, and that covered her face completely.

'This might be a good one to hide behind,' she mused.

'But a mask isn't always to hide behind,' Pietro said, coming to join them. 'Sometimes it can reveal what you never knew before about yourself.'

'That would be the time to beware,' Ruth said. 'You wouldn't know what you were also revealing to other people. They might see you in a way you never dreamed of, and then where would you be?'

'Among friends,' Pietro told her softly. 'And it might be their insight that sets you free.'

Poor Mario looked blankly from one to the other, until rescue came in the form of a customer. Mario hastened to his assistance, but found himself in trouble again. The newcomer was German, speaking no Italian and very little English. Soon there was chaos. Pietro groaned.

'Don't worry,' Ruth told him. 'This is your lucky day.'

'Why?'

'Because you have me,' she said, and walked away before he could reply.

It took her only a few minutes to sort things out, translating the visitor's enquiry, then Mario's response, to the desperate relief of both.

When the satisfied customer had departed, her two companions were loud in their praise.

'My lucky day indeed!' Pietro said. 'Now I remember you said you were a language teacher. *And* you sold him our most expensive package.'

'Mario did that. I was just the conduit.'

'Thank heavens for conduits,' Mario said fervently, and they all laughed.

'We do have an assistant who speaks German,' Mario added, 'but she's only part-time, and not here yet.'

'I think that's worth a coffee and cream cake,' Pietro said. 'Come on.'

They went along the covered passage to the

Café Florian, its elegant interior still reflecting the style of the eighteenth century, when it had first opened.

'Did Gino ever bring you here?' Pietro asked.

'Oh, yes, he told me about Casanova coming here.'

Pietro suppressed the wry comment that this was just what he would have expected. Casanova, the infamous eighteenth-century lover of a thousand women, a man who'd flirted with the church as a career but also flirted with witchcraft. Imprisoned for debt and devil worship, he'd escaped and travelled Europe, pursued by scandal, finally ending his days as a respectable librarian in an obscure castle in Bohemia.

Like many other young men Gino had passed over the respectable part, and used the rest to his advantage.

'He said Casanova came to Florian's because it was the only café in Venice that allowed women inside,' Ruth remembered now.

'Did he say anything else?'

She nodded. 'Lots of things. Some of them were just to make me laugh. Some of them—' She shrugged, with a little sad smile. Then she tensed suddenly. 'No! *No!*'

'What is it?' he asked urgently.

She was pressing her hands to her forehead,

whispering desperately, *'No!'* while Pietro watched her in concern.

Suddenly she gave an exasperated sigh, and dropped her hands.

'It's no good. It's gone. That happens all the time.'

'But it doesn't mean anything. Nobody remembers every detail.'

'I know. I try to tell myself that everyone goes blank sometimes, even normal people.'

'Ruth, you're perfectly normal.'

'No, I'm not. Normal people don't go do-lally in the middle of a conversation.'

'I forbid you to talk like that,' he said in a tight voice.

'All right, not another word, I promise.'

But her easy compliance made him rightly suspicious.

'And I forbid you to *think* it either,' he snapped. 'That's an order.'

'Hey, you're really used to being obeyed, aren't you?'

'Yes, and I expect to be obeyed this time. Don't you ever *dare* call yourself abnormal again.'

Ruth suddenly understood that he was really angry, not just with the exasperated indignation of the day before, but in a mysterious, inexplicable rage.

'Don't you understand why you mustn't think in such a way?' he demanded in a calmer voice.

'I suppose so. But after a while it's natural.'

'Then you've got to stop. I'm going to *make* you stop.'

'Pietro, it's not the same as ordinary forgetfulness. One minute the memories are running through my head, the next—darkness descends. If only I—' She made a helpless gesture.

'Don't try to force it,' he advised her.

'But I'm so close—if I can just—'

'No,' he said, taking her hands in his. 'Let it go. If you fight, it'll fight back. Think of something else—anything else. Find something good and hang on to it.'

There was only him to hang on to, she thought, feeling the warmth of his hands clasping hers. She closed her eyes, willing him to keep her safe, as he was doing now.

'All right?' he asked when she finally looked up.

'Yes, I'm all right now.'

'Did you find something?'

She smiled. 'Yes, I found just what I needed.'

Suddenly her face brightened and she cried, 'Giovanni Soranzo!' in such a voice of triumph that people stared at her.

'Excuse me?' Pietro said.

'You must have heard of him—Doge of Venice, early fourteenth century.'

'Yes, I've heard of him. I'm descended from him.'

'And so is Gino. He told me all about it. That's what I was trying to remember. You were right. When I stopped thinking about it, it came back.'

'Then we've made progress already. Can you remember anything else he said?'

'The Doges ruled Venice for twelve centuries, and were immensely powerful. Gino was so proud of being descended from one of them. He showed me the portrait you keep in the palazzo.'

'We'll have another look at it some time.'

'When we've finished lunch I'd like to wander around a bit on my own.'

'No,' he said at once.

'Yes,' she replied firmly. 'I'm not going to run away again, I promise.'

'You might get lost.'

'You can't get lost in Venice. If you take a wrong turn you just come to the edge and fall into the water. You climb out, soaking wet and cursing horribly, and retrace your steps. You must teach me some of those fine Venetian curses. Gino said they're the best in the world.'

He was forced to laugh at her determined humour.

'I'm safe now, honestly,' she continued. 'I'll

come back to the shop later, and if you're not there I'll make my own way home.'

He agreed but reluctantly, and when they left Florian's his eyes followed her across St Mark's Piazza until she vanished.

It was as well that he returned to the shop, for his part-time assistant didn't show up, and it was a busy afternoon. Late in the day Ruth slipped quietly inside. To his relief she looked calm and cheerful.

He called the palazzo, giving Minna the night off preparing his meal, and on the way home he stopped in several food shops buying fresh meat and vegetables.

'Tonight I do the cooking,' he told Ruth. 'And if that doesn't scare you, nothing will.'

'But Gino said you were a wonderful cook.'

'Compared to him, I was. I enjoy it. And I enjoy surprising people who don't expect me to be able to do it.'

Toni came to meet them as soon as they entered, paying particular attention to Ruth, whom he seemed to consider his particular concern after having guarded her on the first night.

There was a note from Minna on the table, to say that she had taken Toni for a walk and seen him settled before going out for the evening.

'I'd better give him his medication before I start

cooking,' Pietro said. 'Can you hand me the little brown bottle on that shelf behind you?'

Ruth glanced at the label before handing over the bottle, and without thinking, she said, 'Good stuff.'

'You've come across these pills before?' Pietro said quickly. 'When?'

'I—don't know. I just know them. You give them to a dog who has *petit mal*, mild epilepsy.'

'That's right. Perhaps you had a dog of your own?'

'No, I don't think so. My aunt didn't like animals. How often does he have these?'

'Just one a day. Perhaps you can give it to him while I start the food.'

He retreated to the kitchen, but lingered in the doorway, watching as Toni nestled against her, clearly content to trust her. In a few seconds the pill was down.

Her offer to help with the meal was met with lofty dismissal. Women, Pietro gave her to understand, did not belong in the kitchen. While she was still trying to puzzle this out he indicated the china and gave her permission to lay the table.

'Cheek!' she said amiably, and got to work.

Ruth had to admit that he served up a fabulous meal, starting with *risi e bisi,* rice with peas, assuring her that it had been a big favourite with Giovanni Soranzo.

'Oh, yeah!' she said sceptically.

'Listen, you're not talking to Gino now. If I say it, it's true. Well, sort of. Traditionally it was the starter on the Doge's lunch menu every year, during the feast of St Mark.'

'Ah,' Ruth said cunningly, 'but is there any evidence that he actually liked it?'

'He ate it, and it never killed him,' Pietro hedged. 'Why don't you open the wine?'

Although she'd known him such a short time Ruth was coming to treasure these moments of bantering, which took her mind away from problems. She wondered if it did the same for him.

The meal continued with pasta in olive oil, followed by cream cod mousse and sweet biscuits, washed down with light, delicious wines.

Suddenly she said, 'I was going to ask if you've been in touch with Gino since I arrived. But you must have been, and, since you haven't mentioned it, I guess he doesn't want to know.'

Pietro was taken by surprise, but realised that he shouldn't have been. He was getting used to her sharp wits.

'It's not quite like that,' he said cautiously.

'Which means it's exactly like that.'

'He doesn't remember the last evening exactly as you do. He thought you wanted to break up.'

'But how could he?'

'I don't know, but he says you broke up with him.'

She stared, clearly thunderstruck.

'But—but I didn't,' she stammered. 'We had a lovely evening—he said he loved me.' But then her shoulders sagged. 'At least, that's what I remember. But maybe I'm wrong.'

'Maybe you'd had enough of his silly face and wanted something better,' Pietro said kindly, trying to make light of it.

'It doesn't make sense,' she said firmly. 'If I'd changed my mind about him why didn't I tell him on the phone before he ever came to England? Why wait until then?'

'Perhaps you needed to see him to be sure?' Pietro suggested.

'And when I saw him in the restaurant that night I decided against him? But instead I remember how close we were. So I'm imagining that? I'm delusional? Well, there you are. I must be madder than I thought.'

'I told you not to call yourself mad.'

'Well, don't tell me! If I want to abuse myself, I will. Who has a better right?'

He didn't make the mistake of answering, but looked at her wryly until she calmed down and gave a little laugh, aimed at herself.

'I warned you it would be tough,' she said.

'I can take it,' he assured her.

'Which version do you believe?' she challenged. 'His or mine?'

'We both know he didn't always stick to the truth. Look at this.'

He took out the photo albums and went through pages until he found the picture he wanted her to see. It showed Gino with a middle-aged woman. She was wearing an apron, and was busy in a kitchen.

'That was his mother,' Pietro said.

Ruth said nothing for a moment, then, 'Did she work here?'

'Yes, she was our cook for several years. That's how it happened that he grew up here.'

'So he's not your cousin, not a Bagnelli?'

'No, I'm afraid that was one of his fantasies.'

'But I don't understand. I thought you were both descended from the same Doge.'

'That's true, but Doges were elected. It wasn't a hereditary position. There were over a hundred of them, from different families. Almost every true Venetian is descended from one Doge or another.'

'But being a Bagnelli was another of his "fantasies". Or shall we call them lies? When was he going to tell me the truth—if ever? Perhaps Gino himself was an illusion.' She gave a laugh that was almost bitter. 'Maybe he was just a hologram, and if I stretched out my hand it might have gone right through him.'

'I think you've summed him up fairly well,' Pietro said grimly. 'Perhaps it's useful that you're beginning to see him more clearly.'

'But it doesn't change anything. I still need his help, even if I don't—'

'Don't what?' he asked. When she didn't reply he said tensely, 'Do you still love him? Ruth, try to tell me.'

CHAPTER FOUR

'TELL me,' Pietro urged again. 'I know you're trying to be very realistic about everything, but sometimes feelings aren't realistic. After all that's happened—is it possible that you still love him?'

He checked himself, sensing that his voice sounded too intent. Emotional pressure was bad for Ruth. He must try to remember.

'*Can* you still love a man who's treated you in such a way?' he continued more calmly.

'Treated me how? That's what I don't know.'

'He didn't stick around, you know that.'

'But maybe I told him not to, like he said.'

'Maybe.' He didn't sound convinced. 'But what do you feel now?'

She shook her head helplessly.

'How can I tell "then" and "now" apart? I remember how totally I loved him then.'

'And you feel that love now?'

'Yes—no—maybe, but it's really just another

hologram. Press a switch and it would probably vanish. Oh, hell! What's the point of talking? I've got to discover the reality and look it in the eye.' She smiled with a hint of mischief that disturbed his heart. 'Maybe then I'll *spit* in its eye.'

'Reality may hit you harder than you imagine.'

'Then I'll hit back harder still. You don't think I'm going to be beaten by a bit of reality, do you? That to it!' She snapped her fingers.

'Have you ever let anything get the better of you?' he asked, honestly curious.

Making a face full of wicked glee, she replied, 'I don't know. I can't remember.'

She gave a crow of amusement and he joined in, regarding her with admiration. But as his laughter faded hers went on, and there was a note in it that alarmed him.

'Ruth, it's not that funny,' he said gently.

'Yes, it is, it's hilarious. It's the funniest thing that ever happened. Can't you see that?'

'No,' he said, gathering her shaking body into his arms. 'I can see a great many things. You'd be surprised how much I can see. But I can't see that.'

He held her tight, feeling her shaking intensify until he thought her laughter would change into tears. But something else happened. Suddenly she stopped shaking and he felt her shoulders stiffen. Gently but firmly she drew away and disengaged herself, saying in a changed voice, 'OK, I've decided.'

'Why does that scare me?' he asked, trying to make light of it.

'I'm not going to go on like this, living off your charity and wondering if Gino's going to come home, and if he does, will he help me. That's just leaving your fate in someone else's hands, and nuts to it.'

'Good. Keep going.'

'I'm going to get a job, find somewhere to live, make my own way. If Gino comes back, he does. If he doesn't, I'll get on with life some other way.'

'Fine. While you look for a job you can work for me for a while.'

'I said no charity.'

'Will you stop bristling like a hedgehog? You'd be doing me a favour. My other assistant didn't come in today. She's pregnant and having a hard time. If you'll come in for a few weeks I can give her a leave of absence. She'll get the rest she needs, I'll get your language expertise, and everyone's satisfied.'

She thought for a minute.

'And I'll pay you rent?'

'I don't need—'

'It's that or nothing.'

Where did she get the gall to make terms with him? he wondered.

'All right, we'll do it your way.' He added lightly, 'And I'll wager that's something you're used to as well.'

She smiled. 'Who knows?' she said.

'I have a feeling it's going to be interesting finding out.'

When Ruth had gone to bed he sat by the window, looking out at the water, wondering if it had really only been two days since she'd come storming into his life, half drowned, half mad—as she would have put it—totally undefeated. Already it felt like a different universe.

The door opened and Minna looked in.

'Do you want me for anything, signore?'

'No, thank you, Minna. We've done the dishes.'

'I keep asking you not to do that. It's my job.'

'Ruth insisted. You can't argue with her.'

Minna gave him the motherly smile of someone who had worked for his family all her life, and had assumed possessive rights.

'I'm so glad,' she said. 'It's about time.'

'No,' he said hastily. 'Minna, it's not like that.'

'Of course it isn't. I don't mean that at all.'

'Then what?'

'I came in earlier, and as I passed this door I heard you laughing.'

He remembered that Ruth had started to laugh at her own predicament and he'd joined in until amusement had collapsed. But Minna hadn't heard the anguish.

'Do you know how long it's been since you laughed?' Minna asked, regarding him with the fond concern that all his servants felt, although they were careful to hide it.

'A long time,' he agreed. 'But don't—read anything into it.'

'Of course not, signore. It's just that it's nice to hear you laugh again.'

Ruth awoke next day to find a thin strip of brilliant sunlight on the floor. Leaping out of bed, she pulled back the shutters on the windows, and was almost thrown back by the blinding light that streamed in. Rubbing her eyes, she finally managed to look out onto the Grand Canal.

Damp, miserable January seemed to have vanished without a trace. Now the light glittered on the water, showing the great canal snaking away, alive with boats. At this time of day they weren't romantic gondolas but prosaic barges ferrying supplies to shops, hotels and restaurants, and carting rubbish away.

Ruth saw some of them pull into the side at the base of the Rialto Bridge, where people came forward to help unload them and carry their contents up to the shops that lined both sides of the bridge. Instinctively she leaned out and waved to the men on the water, and they waved back, grinning.

Another boat pulled into a small landing-stage by the palazzo, where a tall, powerfully built young man was waiting. Only his back and the top of his head was clearly visible, but Ruth could make out that he was wearing jeans and a tight-fitting short-sleeved vest that showed his muscular arms.

As the boxes were dumped onto the landing-stage he reached for the heaviest one, and hoisted it easily onto his shoulder with a sinuous movement that twisted his whole body, until it straightened up, untroubled by the weight. Ruth smiled, dispassionately admiring the casual display of grace and strength. Then the man raised his head a fraction and she saw that it was Pietro.

He didn't see her, and was gone before she could react. It left her with a strange feeling, as though she'd seen him and not seen him. In a few days of his company she'd perceived him through the prism of her own need, and entirely missed the things that stood out so sharply now.

But this morning, for a split second, she'd had the chance to observe him only as a man, stripped of the irrelevant details that concealed his true self, a man with vibrant physical attractions that made him stand out from other men. The moment had passed and he was Count Bagnelli again, but the memory remained, a source of mysterious pleasure. She tucked it away for future consideration.

To her eyes the whole world was bright, alive, hopeful, and it perfectly matched her mood. Last night she'd come to a resolution, to take her fate in her own hands. It had made her feel reborn, and now she could almost imagine that Venice was doing its best to encourage her.

I'm just being fanciful, she thought. *I've got to stop that.*

But she remembered Pietro saying how Venetians were like a family, offering a generous welcome. Perhaps she wasn't being so fanciful after all.

By the time she joined Pietro he was more soberly dressed, ready for the shop.

'I'm a new woman,' she informed him. 'And I'm going to do something spectacular to prove it.'

'What?' he asked, grinning.

'Switch on my cell phone,' she declared with a comical air of anticlimax.

'It's been off all this time?'

'I switched it off at the airport in England, and since then I've had other things on my mind. Now's the time to find out that all the mighty of the world have been queuing up to talk to me. Oh!' She stared at the screen.

'Anyone mighty?' he asked.

'The publisher who's been giving me work. I sent him a book I'd translated from Spanish into English about a week ago. It's surely too soon for a reaction.'

But the text message was, *'Vital you call at once.'*

There were two other texts in increasing agitation.

'I must have made some ghastly error,' Ruth said worriedly.

'Don't jump to conclusions,' Pietro advised her.

'But it's obvious. There was me, thinking I was doing so well and I was making a foul up all the time.'

Pietro took her by the shoulders and gave her a gentle shake.

'Hey, steady on. You don't know any of this. Don't put yourself down. You're a new woman today, remember?'

'That's a joke. I've been fooling myself.'

'And I say you haven't. Now, stop panicking, call him and find out what he wants.'

As before she felt herself growing steady under his influence.

'Right,' she said. 'Fine.'

'Use my phone,' he suggested suddenly, picking up the receiver. 'Give me the number.'

She did so and he dialled, giving her the receiver. After a minute a man's voice answered.

'Hallo, Jack? It's me? What did I do wrong?'

Before Jack could answer Pietro reached forward and pressed the loudspeaker button on the phone so that Jack's voice boomed out for him to hear.

'Wrong? Nothing. Everything's fine. Señor Salvatore is well pleased. He's a very difficult man, you know. His books have to be translated perfectly, or else! The book you did is the first in a trilogy, and he wants you to do the other two.'

Pietro gave her a thumbs up, and she beamed at him.

'I've been going crazy,' Jack continued, 'not able to get hold of you, and him screeching that it's you or nobody. Now I can get back to him and tell him that you've agreed to do them.'

Pietro shook his head.

'But I haven't agreed,' Ruth said, taking her cue from him.

Jack's reply was almost a yelp. 'Yes, you have, you have, *you have!* Please, Ruth, don't argue. Think of my blood pressure. You've already given it a bad time.'

'No, Jack, I'm giving it a very good time,' she responded with spirit. 'I'm the answer to your prayers, remember?'

'Only if you say yes.'

'I'm thinking about it.' Seeing Pietro make a

gesture of rubbing his fingers against his thumb, she added, 'What about money?'

'I'll up the money.'

'Double it,' Ruth said remorselessly.

'One and a half.'

'Double. You need me, remember?'

'Anything, anything. Will you be home soon?'

'No, I'm staying in Venice a while. You can send the books to the Palazzo Bagnelli.' To Pietro she mouthed, 'What's the full address?'

He gave it to her and she passed it on to Jack, who assured her that the two books would be on their way to her immediately.

'And the money for the one I've just finished,' she reminded him. 'That'll be in my bank account any day now, won't it?

He groaned. 'You drive a hard bargain.'

'Of course. I'm the best.'

She switched off and looked up to find Pietro's eyes meeting hers. Together they crowed, *'Yes!'*

'You cheeky so-and-so,' she reproved him. 'That's why you wanted me to use your phone.'

'I'm merely concerned for your welfare.'

'You merely wanted a good snoop.'

'They can be hard to tell apart,' he conceded. 'I'm used to worrying about you. I can't just stop.'

'I guess I don't really want you to stop. I could

still fall flat on my face, and who'll pick me up, if not you?'

'As long as that's understood. I'm Chief Picker Upper—until you no longer need one.'

'That's a long way off,' she said, suddenly serious. 'The new woman is only skin deep, for the moment.'

'I hope this doesn't mean you won't have any time for me. I could really do with you in the shop.'

'I still want to work there. I can translate in the evenings. When do I start?'

'How about this morning?' His tone became joking again. 'I'd better get some work out of you before the rest of the world beats a path to your door.'

'They want me,' she breathed. 'They want me and nobody else.'

'Of course they do. You're the best. They know that because you told them.'

Ruth aimed a swipe at him and he ducked, grinning. Minna, entering at that moment, nodded as though she'd seen something that confirmed what she already believed. Understanding her, Pietro grimaced, wishing it were possible to explain that she'd got it wrong. Ruth had reached out to him in her need and vulnerability, and in caring for her he'd found a strange kind of peace. But he knew Minna would never understand this.

Like everyone who worked for him she was just waiting to celebrate the day when he found another wife and emerged from the darkness that too often engulfed him. But none of them understood how far from happening that was, and how determined he was to keep a distance between himself and all women.

Ruth was different. Her unique situation meant he could care for her without dread of the outcome.

By now Ruth was beginning to know the way to St Mark's, down this *calle*, across that little square, across a bridge, until they came out near the cathedral and crossed the piazza to the shop.

Mario, forewarned of her arrival, was lyrical in his relief. Together he and Pietro showed her the ropes, but then Pietro wisely stood back and let them put their heads together. Free from his employer's eye, Mario admitted that his French was patchy.

'I just about get by,' he said, 'and so far there have been no disasters, but if you—'

He broke off with a pleading look.

'Don't worry,' she told him, smiling. 'French is one of my languages.'

But her first chance to prove her worth came, not with a foreign language, but with an Englishman who spoke with a strong regional accent. Seeing Mario floundering Ruth stepped in, becoming a conduit again until the man was out of the shop.

'He said he spoke English,' Mario protested.

'He did,' Ruth said. 'But you have to come from a certain part of England to understand it. Never mind. We sold him an expensive package, and that's what really matters.'

'Spoken like a true entrepreneur,' Pietro said appreciatively.

'You have a gift for finance,' Mario agreed.

'I never knew that before. I'm just a language teacher—why, that's it! *That's it!*'

She struck her head and did a little dance of delight.

'Now I remember, I was friendly with one of the other teachers, and I used to visit her at home. She had a dog with epilepsy.'

'That's excellent,' Pietro said. 'Bit by bit, we'll win. Now you and Mario had better go off and have lunch together before we confuse the poor fellow any more.'

From the first she'd been at ease with Mario. Over lunch she explained briefly that her memory was sometimes vague, owing to an accident. There was no need to mention Gino.

'That's why some of the things you hear me say don't seem to make sense,' she said.

'Like about the dog? Thank you for telling me.'

He told her about his life, which might be described as sedate. He still lived with his family, under his mother's thumb from the sound of it. He'd worked in the shop for five years and his admiration for Count Bagnelli was enormous.

'Mind you, he'd be annoyed if he heard me call him that,' Mario admitted. 'He never uses the title if he can avoid it. In fact I think he actually dislikes it, says it's more trouble than it's worth.'

'Now that sounds like an affectation,' Ruth said decidedly.

'Oh, no, he's never gone in for a lot of display. He started the business because he preferred to work for a living. He doesn't consider administering his estate working.'

'You mean, he doesn't have to do it?' Ruth asked. 'I thought the Bagnellis must have lost all their money.'

'He's one of the richest men in Italy.'

'But that great empty palace is like a building that's been abandoned and left to rot.'

Mario shook his head vigorously.

'You can't have seen much of it, or you wouldn't say that. It's kept in perfect condition. Any crack is mended at once, before it can spread. Every piece of furniture is protected by dust covers. But it's empty, except for a few rooms where he lives alone, or as much alone as he can manage. There used to be dozens of servants in the palazzo, but he sent them to work on his estate, and shut most of the rooms up.'

He gave an envious sigh.

'You should have seen it ten years ago, when the old count was still alive. He was a man who enjoyed the high life, and Pietro was the same. The reputation he had! Casanova lived again! I was in my teens and I lapped up the stories. I swore I'd be the same when I was older but—'

He shrugged and looked down at his unimpressive person. Ruth smiled in sympathy.

'So Pietro had a big reputation with women?' she said curiously.

'The biggest,' said a voice just behind her, and Ruth turned to see a large middle-aged woman with a motherly face.

'Hallo, Jessica,' Mario greeted her. 'This is Ruth who's coming to work in the shop. Jessica owns this place.'

When greetings had been exchanged Jessica got back to the subject that clearly fascinated her.

'I've lived in Venice all my life, and you never saw anything like it. There wasn't a woman in town who wouldn't have taken him to her bed. But he only slept with the best, very stylish ladies.'

'I suppose they were all aristocrats, like him,' Ruth suggested.

'No!' Both her companions shook their heads vigorously as though to advance such an idea was to miss the point.

'He didn't care about titles,' Jessica said. 'Why should he, when he has one of his own? But they had to be outstanding, not just beautiful, but with a certain "something extra", to make him proud.'

It was clear that she considered Pietro a credit to Venice.

'The Palazzo Bagnelli was the best place in town to be entertained,' Mario agreed.

'They took on extra staff for parties,' Jessica added. 'I've worked there myself many times.'

'But now there's only Minna and Celia,' Mario observed, 'and people say he only keeps them out of kindness, that he'd prefer to be completely alone.'

'But how can any man live like that?' Ruth wondered. 'And why?'

'It's been that way since his wife died. She loved entertaining too. The place was always full of people and light. Then she died and the lights went out.'

'I knew he was a widower,' Ruth says, 'but he avoids all mention of her. What was she like?'

But before he could answer there was a cry of 'Hey, Mario!' from a couple of his friends who had come in, and in the flurry of introductions the subject was lost.

Ruth was left wondering. There were so many

things she wanted to ask about Pietro, but everything she learned only seemed to deepen the mystery. It was impossible to connect the light-hearted playboy of Jessica and Mario's description with the man who now lived like a monk in dark solitude.

She took some papers home to continue studying the firm. Pietro explained a good deal to her, and they spent a pleasant evening working. But when she'd gone to bed she remembered how Mario had said she couldn't have seen much of the palazzo. Gino had taken her over the building, showing it off with a proprietorial air that she now realised had been part of his performance. She hadn't noticed much about the condition of the place. She had been too dazzled by the young man.

Now she realised how little she'd thought of him today. Pietro had occupied her thoughts more. Mario's words, 'Then she died and the lights went out,' were haunting.

The building had never seemed so dark and silent, as though the man whose heart had died with his wife had turned it into a tomb, where he could wait until the day he would be with her.

She went to the window, looking out to where the landing-stage bobbed in the water just below her, then ran her eyes down the length of the building, until they fixed on a portion that jutted out slightly with windows on three sides.

She blinked, wondering if she had only imagined the man standing there. But no, it was Pietro.

Why did he go to that part of the house? What had happened to draw him to that room at night, and what made him stand there, so deadly still?

She thought of the night when he had rescued her, and her heart went out to him, looking so much in need of rescue himself. Putting on a loose robe, she slipped out into the corridor and turned in the direction that she guessed he was.

There were no lights here, just the reflection of the canal coming through the windows at the end of the corridor. Dimly she could make out the great marble staircase leading down, and she began to descend, her bare feet making no noise.

When she was nearly at the bottom she saw that a large double door was open, and turned towards the room beyond, which she could just make out was a nursery, with an elaborate cradle in the corner. This was where his child would have slept, if it had lived.

Pietro was there, standing by the window, so still that he might have turned to stone. This was the second time today that she had watched him unaware, she realised. But how different from this morning when she'd seen him at his handsome, athletic best. Now he looked like the loneliest man on earth, and she longed to go in and speak to him, but lacked the courage. When he turned she stepped back, keeping out of sight.

He walked out, moving heavily, and she retreated farther into the darkness, knowing that she must not invade his solitude, and there was nothing that she, or anyone else, could say to him. He passed on without noticing her.

CHAPTER FIVE

IT HAD been agreed between them that Ruth would not go to the shop next day, but remain at home studying papers. Pietro left early and she ate breakfast alone, still brooding over what she had seen the night before.

He was the strong one, needing and wanting nothing from her, except perhaps that her company was less demanding than anyone else's. He'd encouraged her to lean on him, because that was the kind of man he was.

But always he kept her at a slight distance, ready to be offended if she offered him warmth or help. He preferred to give comfort rather than receive it. He felt safer that way. In many ways it was an attractive trait, making him a generous friend, but it was also a subtle way of protecting his isolation.

It was that instinctive understanding that had made her keep back in the shadows the night before, leaving him to the solitude he preferred and from which she was excluded. It was a rejection and, mysteriously, it hurt.

Remembering what Mario and Jessica had told her, she became curious about the great building that surrounded her. Last year Gino had shown her around, but it had been a hurried visit to the most grandiose parts, always avoiding the servants.

'We don't want prying eyes,' he'd whispered.

Of course not, she thought now. He didn't want them revealing his deception.

There was still much to be seen, and when she was sure that Minna and Celia were out she went exploring.

What she discovered was awesome. This was a palace in fact as well as in name, a glorious edifice in the grand manner, with vast rooms and flowing staircases, the high vaulted ceilings carved with an intricacy that was surely impossible.

Yet there was another story being told as well. Often she could see where pictures had been hung on the wall and then removed, leaving pale spaces. Presumably they were in storage.

Down one long upstairs corridor she found salon after salon, which must once have been the waiting rooms of those waiting to see the great man. All, now, were bleak and anonymous.

She meant not to intrude on the lord's bedroom,

even though Pietro wasn't occupying it now. But she came upon it by accident, opening a small door in the last salon, which looked as though it led only to a cupboard. Then she stood on the threshold, dumbfounded.

Certainly here was no hint of privacy, only a gigantic bed, hung with curtains that swept up to a coronet. It wasn't a bed for lovers, but an arena where the count and countess would perform their duty to ensure the succession. Duty done, they could then turn away and sleep six feet apart.

There were no bedclothes, only the bare mattress, looking hard and uncomfortable. Every surface in the room was clear. Nowhere could she see photographs or anything personal. Ruth understood that no man would choose to live here if he could escape, but the absence of all human trace suggested something more disturbing.

Pietro wasn't just grieving for his dead wife. He was so devastated that he'd withdrawn from the luxury he'd taken for granted all his life, to exist like a monk in a cell. He could barely be said to be living in the palazzo at all, since she was sure their little apartment actually formed part of the servants' quarters. Her brief glimpses of the little room where he slept had revealed that it was severely functional and far less comfortable than her own.

Wandering slowly around, she passed a long

mirror and caught a glimpse of herself. Shocked, she stared at herself, forgetting everything else.

'Son of a pig!' she muttered, using one of Pietro's favourite curses. 'I look *terrible!*'

It was a sight she must have seen before, but it had never made the impact of today. Her dress had been bought before she lost weight, and hung on her awkwardly, doing nothing to make her attractive. Her hair was nondescript, worn short because that was easiest. For a year she hadn't bothered with make-up.

Moving slowly, she went to stand before the mirror, facing the dismal truth head on.

'Hmm!' she thought. 'So much for new woman.'

Then energy returned and she was out of the door, running the length of the building until she reached her room, where she checked her purse, found her bank card and fled outside. A few minutes at the cash machine showed that the money Jack owed her for the first book was safely deposited. Since he wasn't known for swift payment she concluded, with a little smile, that she mattered more to him than even he had admitted.

By now she was beginning to be familiar with the narrow streets and was able to find her way easily to a dress shop she'd noticed before. One glance at her slender figure and the assistants fell on her with delight. When she left she bore with her four dresses, two pairs of fashionable jeans, three sweaters, a variety of dainty underwear and the address of 'the best hairdresser in town'.

'It's actually so short that I don't think there's much you can do with it,' she told the hairdresser apologetically.

She was wrong. After two hours her blunt, prosaic hair was transformed into an elegant confection with just enough curve and bounce to give it life.

She could have walked straight back home, but some impulse made her turn her steps in the direction of St Mark's, and then into the shop.

'Just one moment, signorina,' Mario said, scribbling something. At last he looked up. 'Now, what can I—?' His voice faded as he looked at her.

At last he managed to stammer, 'You—you—' and left it there, his jaw dropping.

Laughing, she reached out and raised it again with her fingers. Neither of them saw Pietro appear from the back of the shop and stand watching, his eyes fixed on Ruth.

'Is something wrong?' she teased Mario, charmed by his innocent reaction.

'No, it's just—Ruth? You're Ruth?'

'You mustn't ask her that question, Mario,' came a voice from the shadows. 'It's dangerous.'

They both turned and saw Pietro, who came forward slowly.

'I don't understand,' Mario said.

'It doesn't matter,' Ruth said. 'We just talk in riddles. I'm delighted you didn't recognise me.'

'Of course I know girls like to change their appearance,' Mario said, trying to sound worldly-wise, 'but this—you're transformed.'

'Maybe it's about time,' she said quietly, her eyes on Pietro.

'You'll certainly attract the customers,' he agreed.

There was something in his voice that set her at a slight distance, and she was sure of it a moment later when he said, 'Why don't you go on home? Tell Minna I'll be late. I've got things to catch up with here.'

'Can I help?'

'No need,' he said briefly. 'You go on. I'll see you later.'

He finished the conversation by walking away, leaving her nothing to do but go.

Pietro was late home, and she told herself that she was glad of it because it left her free to work on learning Italian. She'd bought a book and some tapes, and needed to practise her pronunciation in privacy.

When she'd had enough of that she went into her room and took another look at the clothes that she'd put up on hangers. At last she selected a dress cut on deceptively simple lines, but actually something that only a woman with a perfect figure could risk.

Regarding herself in the tall mirror, she knew she was one of those very women. But that was small comfort when she was standing here alone. Pietro had suddenly decided to stay away this evening of all evenings.

What would Gino think if he could see her now?

And did it matter?

She sighed, turning to move away from the mirror. Then she saw Pietro standing there.

'You left your door open,' he said by way of apology.

'I was just giving myself a conceited moment,' she said with a little laugh that sounded oddly embarrassed to her own ears.

'I'm glad. You've earned it. What suddenly prompted you to do this?'

'Partly it came from last night. When you get sick of being a permanent invalid, buying new clothes is the right thing to do.'

He came to stand behind her, looking at her reflection, which showed an elegant woman with a touch of sophistication, something Ruth was sure she had never been before. But she liked it.

'Let me introduce you to Ruth Three,' she said, indicating the mirror.

'Three?' he asked cautiously.

'For years I was Ruth One, but now she's gone and I'm even glad to be rid of her. She was boring and stupid, easily taken in.'

'She was generous and trusting,' Pietro corrected gently. 'She believed the man she loved.'

'Exactly. Like I said, stupid. Then she turned into Ruth Two. She's the one who arrived here the other night.'

'Don't say anything against her,' Pietro warned.

'I'm not going to. It wasn't her fault that she was the way she was, but, let's face it, it didn't make her very good company.'

'I liked her company,' he observed quietly. 'She was easy to talk to, and she gave back more than she knew.'

'You're just being kind. I'd had enough of her. I'm ready for Ruth Three.'

'And what is she like?'

'I have no idea, that's the best of it. I never met her before today, but I think she's been waiting to appear for some time. I'll tell you this, she's not just going to sit there and take it like the other two.'

'Just the same, they had something that mattered. Don't change too much.'

She put her head on one side, then the other. Then she brushed her fingers through the front hairs where they fell over her forehead. This way, then that way.

'I can't decide,' she said.

'Let me see.'

He turned her to him and touched her forehead gently. But then he stopped, for his fingers had brushed against a scar, the last reminder of her injuries.

'I'm sorry,' he whispered.

'It doesn't hurt anymore,' she assured him. 'That's all in the past.'

But it wasn't in the past. It was still here and now, despite the new appearance and the burst of confidence.

'Does it show very much?' she asked.

'No, just a thin line. You'd never see it—unless you already knew it was there.'

'That's the way to be,' she said softly. 'Keep the pain to yourself, unless you find someone else who understands.'

He nodded. 'You're right, although not everyone is that lucky.'

He brushed her few hairs back and leaned down, gently laying his lips against the scar.

'It's going to be all right,' he whispered.

They settled into a comfortable routine. Pietro gave Ruth a key to the side door, making her independent. Most days she went to the shop with him. At other times she stayed at home studying papers, brushing up on her Italian, sometimes going for walks, learning about Venice as she'd never done before. In Gino's company she'd thought only of Gino, but now she began to love the little city for its own sake.

Stripped of tourists, it contained barely seventy thousand people, 'true Venetians' who thought their unique home the most perfect place on earth, no matter how difficult and impractical life might become.

There were no cars, so that people either went by boat or walked. Even an elevator could be a luxury.

'We can't install elevators,' Mario told her. 'The buildings are so old and frail that the vibration would make everything fall down. My grandparents have to climb seventy steps to get from the ground to their apartment at the top of the building.'

'Wouldn't they be better off somewhere else?'

He stared at her in amazement.

'They're Venetian,' he said, as though that explained everything. And Ruth guessed that it did.

Sometimes she helped Mario with his English, sometimes he helped her with her Italian.

'But you'll also need to know Venetian dialect,' he told her once. 'Have you noticed the sign outside the shop? "*Qua se parla anca in Veneto.*" It means "Here we also speak Venetian". Not everyone does, and we're very proud of it.'

'I guess I can manage,' Ruth said cheerfully. 'We have dialects in my country too. Remember that man?'

'The one you helped me with? Yes, but he only pronounced English words in his own way. Venetian is a completely different language.'

'Oh, yes,' she said slowly as something cropped up in her mind. 'Venetian has the letter "j", which you never find in Italian.'

'That's true,' Mario said. 'So you already know about our dialect?'

'A little,' she murmured. 'I remember about the "j".'

How Gino had chuckled the day he said, *'Ti voglio bene.'* It means "I wish you well",' he'd explained. 'But it's how Italians say "I love you."'

'I don't believe it. It's so sedate.'

'But we are sedate,' he'd said in mock indignation. 'A very sedate, proper people. We say *"Ti voglio bene."* Unless we are Venetian, and then we say, *"Te voja ben."*'

Gino's words whispered through her head. *Te voja ben—te voja ben.*

But suddenly there was another memory fluttering at the edge of her mind, refusing to let her seize it but also refusing to go away. It was more recent—he had said these words to her and she had said them back to him again and again, holding him close in an ecstasy of love. Just a few days ago—but that was impossible—if only she could remember—

'Ruth, are you all right?' Mario asked anxiously.

'Yes, I'm fine,' she said hastily.

The memory vanished. She sighed and let it go. It had escaped anyway.

A few days later she was working in the back with Pietro when Mario put his head around the door.

'Ruth, there's a man out here who's looking for you.'

She drew a sharp breath. Gino must have returned. Who else would be looking for her? But then she remembered that Mario knew Gino and would have said it was him. Conscious of Pietro's eyes upon her, she asked, 'Did he give his name?'

'Señor Salvatore Ramirez.'

'What? But he's the man whose books I'm translating. Let me see.'

She darted past him into the front of the shop. Pietro, following more slowly, was just in time to see an extravagantly handsome man approach her with a theatrical gesture.

'I have brought the books myself because I had to meet the lady who understands my writing better than anyone in the world,' he declared expansively, speaking in Spanish. 'I called first at your address but they told me to come here.'

'You're very kind,' she murmured.

'And now tell me that I can take you away. We will spend the evening together, talking about many things you need to know to help you with the other books. I will open my heart to you, you will open your heart to me, and in the joy of mutual understanding we will create a work of art.'

'Well, there are some questions I'd like to discuss with you,' she mused. 'Pietro, is it all right if I go? Señor Ramirez says—'

'Yes, I understood quite as much as I wanted,' Pietro said in disgust. 'Get him out of here.'

'I don't suppose I'll be very late—'

'Be as late as you please, but go before I throw up.'

Ruth returned to the palazzo in the early hours, having enjoyed one of the best evenings of her life. She slipped in quietly, prepared to creep up to her room, but Pietro was lying on the sofa with his feet up and a baleful expression on his face.

'Is this what you call not being very late?'

'Is it late? I hadn't noticed.'

'Too busy creating a work of art?' he asked ironically.

'Something like that.'

Her eyes were bright with champagne, but also with an evening's pleasure. She threw herself into a chair, stretching luxuriously.

'Oh, what an evening! I learned so much.'

'Good,' he said briefly.

'I hope you didn't wait up for me.'

'I was a little concerned for you. I shouldn't have let you go off with him like that. He might have been any kind of a bad character.'

'No, he's charming. It was a wonderful night.'

'I didn't think restaurants stayed open this late.'

'It didn't. They threw us out, so we went back to his hotel.'

'And stayed there for several hours,' he said grimly.

'Really?' She looked at her watch, apparently startled. 'Oh, yes, I didn't notice the time.'

'So you had such a good time that now you're full of ideas for translating his books?' Pietro's voice had a touch of sarcasm.

'Yes, I—oh, heavens! The books.' This time her alarm was genuine.

'Where are they?'

'I must have left them in the hotel room. I've got to go back. How did I manage to forget them?'

'I can't imagine,' Pietro said dryly.

At that moment there came the sound of the bell from the side door down below. Exchanging glances, they went to the window and looked out. There stood Salvatore, accompanied by a beautiful woman in her forties.

'Ruth,' she called up merrily. 'You left the books behind.' She held them up.

'Amanda, I'm so sorry,' Ruth called.

'I'll come down and let you in,' Pietro said.

'No, no, we can't stay,' Amanda called. 'We leave early tomorrow morning and we must get some sleep. I'll leave the books here on the ground. Goodbye.'

She and Salvatore blew kisses and vanished into the night, arms about each other. Pietro hurried down and collected the books.

'Don't lose them again,' he said, giving them to Ruth. 'And who is Amanda?'

'His wife, of course. Isn't she sweet?'

'His wife?'

'Yes.'

'She's been with you all the time?' Pietro asked slowly.

'Of course. Actually I learned more from her than from him. I think she helps to write the books, or even writes most of them. She's probably the one who insisted on having me to translate.'

'Does Ramirez do anything himself?'

'Well, he tells very good funny stories. I've never laughed so much as I did tonight—at least, I don't think I have. But like many men, he's chiefly window-dressing.' She yawned. 'Now I must go to bed. Goodnight.' When he didn't answer she raised her voice. 'Goodnight, Pietro.'

He jumped. 'What?'

'I said goodnight, but you were staring into the distance. Did you hear me?'

'No—yes—goodnight.'

She smiled as she went into her room. For reasons she couldn't have explained, she had enjoyed the last few minutes more than she would have thought possible.

Now her days were pleasantly full, either working at the shop or sitting up late working on the books she was translating. Ruth clung to her resolve not to brood about Gino, and found that it worked better that way. Odd snippets did come back to her, to be fitted, piece by piece, into the wall that her mind was gradually building up. It helped, but it wasn't a final answer.

'Perhaps there won't be a final answer,' she mused to herself. 'Maybe I'll just have to remake my life from here.'

Once that thought would have scared her, but now she could consider the prospect calmly, even deal with it. In Venice she'd found the last thing she'd ever dared to hope for: safety. It had something to do with Pietro, whose steadying hand was always held out to her.

She found it easy to get on with his associates, particularly Barone Franco Farini, a big, bouncing man who'd started as a porter, made a fortune out of kitchen utensils and was now anxious to 'better himself'. To this end he'd bought a palace on one of the islands in the lagoon and managed to get a defunct title of nobility revived and attached to himself.

Among his other acquisitions was a much younger wife who'd married him for his spurious title and liked nothing better than to prance around in what she felt was his glory.

Ruth found that it was hard to take seriously a man so naively pleased with his toys, but there was something charming about his innocence and open-heartedness.

'How did he ever make a fortune in big business?' she chuckled after their first meeting.

'By using a completely different part of his brain,' Pietro said with a grin. 'The business part is tough as old boots, and none too scrupulous. The bit that went gaga for Serafina is just plain thick. Since you're a language expert, you probably know the derivation of the term "Barone"?'

'Its Latin root is "bara", meaning simpleton,' she said, laughing. 'Poor Franco.'

'It will be poor Franco when Serafina leaves him and demands millions.'

'You don't know that she'll do that.'

'You haven't met her,' Pietro replied ominously.

Part of Franco's plan to better himself was to improve his English, which was terrible. To this end he engaged Ruth in long, eager conversations about his island and the spectacular party he was planning there during Carnival, and for which Pietro was selling the tickets.

'It will be big, big, big,' he explained. 'Everybody will be there—all the big people. We all go over the water in gondolas, and there is my Serafina looking more beautiful than any other woman.'

'He's spent a fortune in jewels for her, and she can't wait to show them off,' Pietro observed later. 'And that's in addition to the other fortune that he's spending on the rest of the party.'

'Are you going?'

Pietro shuddered.

'Definitely not. I've given him as much advice as I can, which was only fair considering what a profit I've made from the tickets. But all that noisy jollity isn't for me. I guess I'm getting old.'

He looked anything but old. He was dressed as he had been the morning she'd watched him lifting the box from the boat, and seen him simply as a man. And, viewed dispassionately, he was a man to take the shine out of other men, at the height of his strength and masculine beauty, yet seemingly oblivious. Nobody could be more careless where his own attractions were concerned, and that was almost the greatest attraction of all.

Yet it was only half the story, she knew. No woman could live as close to him as she did and not see that inside him everything was different. The 'other' Pietro shunned the world, because only in that way could he find peace, albeit a bleak, arid peace. And she thought the contrast between his two selves explained why he sometimes gave the impression of living on the edge of a volcano.

CHAPTER SIX

FOR the next few days Pietro was mostly silent, and then one afternoon he paused in the shop doorway and said, 'I've just got to run an errand across town.'

'I'll come with you,' Ruth said. 'I need a walk.'

'Not this time,' he said quietly. 'I'm leaving right now.'

'I'm ready now.'

'I said no. I'll see you later.'

He left quickly, before she could reply, and it took a moment for her to realise that she had been snubbed.

'Don't mind too much,' Mario said. 'I think he must be going to San Michele. That's a little island in the lagoon, and it's the Venetian cemetery. His wife and child are buried there. He goes over every month. He never says anything but I always know because he's very quiet on those days.'

'Oh, goodness!' Ruth groaned. 'I'm so clumsy.'

'No, how could you have known?'

'You started to tell me about his wife once, but we were interrupted. Did you ever meet her?'

'Oh, yes, several times. Her name was Lisetta Allucci. She and Pietro had grown up together, She used to come in here a lot, a very nice lady. Everyone was happy for them when they got engaged, and then she became pregnant at once, which was wonderful because he would have an heir.'

'Do people still think like that nowadays?'

'They do if they have a title. The count must have an heir. They were married in St Mark's, and all Venice was there. You never saw such a happy couple, how proudly they walked down the aisle. But they hardly had any time together, just two years. She lost the baby, but soon she was pregnant again. This time the child was born, but she died the same day, and the baby died within a few hours. They were buried together, the child lying in his mother's arms.'

Horror held Ruth silent. She had known that Pietro was a man haunted by tragedy, but it was a shock to hear the cruel details spelt out. She saw him, living almost alone in that great echoing palazzo, shunning human company to be alone with his memories.

'And I barged in,' she murmured. 'Just like I tried to barge in just now. How does he put up with me?'

Now she remembered how grimly he reacted to any mention of those he'd lost, walking away as though unable to bear the reminder.

She was ready for him to be in a bad mood when he reached home that evening, but the hours passed with no sign of him.

'I suppose I ought to go to bed,' she mused to Toni, who eyed her without comment.

'But I expect you'd like a walk, wouldn't you?' she suggested. 'Come on, we'll take a little stroll.'

They would just drift quietly around the local *calles,* she told herself. There was no need to go far, in case she got lost. And if she happened to see Pietro along the way, that would just be a coincidence.

But he was nowhere to be seen, and at last the two of them wandered back to the empty house, and let themselves quietly in. Pietro still wasn't home, so she put some fresh water down for Toni and went to bed.

Where had he gone when he'd left his wife's grave? Had he walked around the city, revisiting the places they had been together, just as she did with her memories of Gino? Only in his case the impressions would be more vivid because the reality had been fulfilment, even though it had ended in tragedy.

Lying there, listening to the echoing silence,

Ruth knew that Lisetta's real tomb was this house. Its very emptiness was a shrine to her memory, an outward symbol of the desolation within, his way of telling the world that she had been the love of his life, and there would never be another.

She listened long and hard, but never hearing the sound of his key, until at last she slept, and awoke next morning to find him still missing. Nor did he appear at the shop all day. He was there when she went home, but he only nodded briefly and shut himself into his room, from where she heard the click of his computer.

She thought of knocking on his door later to ask if he wanted some coffee, but backed off, lacking the courage.

The next day he was back to his usual self. He never mentioned his dark mood, and nor did she.

A few afternoons later, when darkness had fallen early, as it did in January, she found Mario gazing up into the sky where the moon glimmered. Interpreting this as romantic yearning, she said kindly, 'It's a beautiful moon, isn't it?'

'Oh, yes,' he sighed. 'And it will be a full moon any day now, unfortunately.'

'Unfortunately? Isn't a full moon beautiful?'

'Not when it brings *aqua alta,*' Mario said promptly.

'That's high water, isn't it? Flooding.'

'That's right. Venice is flooded about four times a year, and sometimes it happens at full moon, because of the tides. We might be in for it soon.' He shivered.

'Not nice?' she hazarded.

'Everywhere you go you have to walk on planks over the water, and it's always crowded, so that you fall off and get your feet wet. Brr!'

So much for romantic yearning, she thought, with wry amusement. That would teach her to jump to conclusions. But then Mario added wistfully, 'Don't worry, you won't get pushed off. Everyone will make way for you.'

Since her transformation he'd made no effort to hide his admiration. Nor did other men. Wherever she went she received the homage of lingering looks, except from Pietro. True, he studied her appearance, but only to tell her gruffly to keep warm.

The incident sharpened her eyes, and as she walked home that night she realised that the city was full of people studying the sky. Pietro too halted as they were crossing a tiny bridge over a narrow 'backstreet' canal, and looked up.

'Do you think we're going to have *aqua alta?*' she asked him.

'So you're learning to be a Venetian?'

'Mario was telling me about how it's connected to full moon.'

'Or new moon. It can be either. This one was new about ten days ago. The water didn't rise then, but there's been a lot of rain recently. It'll be a relief when full moon is over.'

'Does it worry you very much?' she asked as they walked on. 'I suppose it damages the buildings?'

'It can if they're not properly cared for. I've had all the floors at ground level inside the palazzo raised, and we're well supplied with sandbags, but some people are surprisingly careless.'

'But do you have time to put in sandbags?'

'Yes, because sirens start blaring out a few hours before, so we get some warning.'

When they reached home he showed her the raised floors and she realised that she'd always been vaguely puzzled at having to step up from the street.

'I had all the marble and mosaic taken up,' he explained, 'then three layers of brick laid down, and the floor relaid on top of them. It protects us against many of the floods, which usually aren't more than a couple of inches. But nothing could have protected us against this.'

He pointed to a line on the wall, about six feet up.

'That's how high the water came in nineteen sixty-six,' he said. 'My father always refused to clean that mark off. He said it must be a warning to us never to be complacent about what the sea could do.'

'You mean it could be that bad again?'

'I doubt it. Such a flood will happen only once in a hundred years. But my father was right about not being always on our guard.'

'The water came up that high?' she murmured, running her finger along the line.

'All through the house. Come and see.'

He began to lead her the length of the building. Although these walls had been cleaned they all bore the faint line with its warning for those who could understand.

'Did Gino show you this?' Pietro asked.

'We walked through it quickly, but it was the rooms upstairs he wanted to show me.'

'Ah, yes. It's a lot finer up there,' he said lightly.

Instead of the back stairs that they usually used he led her to the main staircase, a marble edifice wide enough for four people abreast, and from there into the great ballroom, where he switched on the lights.

This was truly the centre of a palace. The ceiling soared, here and there were exquisite carvings, and although most pictures had been put into storage there were still one or two portraits on the walls.

'My ancestors,' Pietro said. 'That one over there is Giovanni Soranzo.'

'I don't like the look of him much,' she said, regarding the man with the scowling face and magnificent robes, who looked down on them in haughty disapproval.

'Not a nice character,' he agreed. 'He locked his daughter up so securely that she didn't get out until seven years after his death.'

'Charming.'

She continued her wandering. One wall was lined with tall windows, each with a little balcony, looking out over the Grand Canal.

Then something in her mind clicked, but silently, and she was back in another time.

'This is where we'll have our wedding reception, cara.'

'But it's much too grand for me.'

'Nothing is too good for you. I shall show you off with such pride.'

And she had believed him.

'Are you all right?' Pietro asked, watching her face.

'Yes, just remembering. Gino talked about having our reception here.'

'You would have done. It was going to be my wedding gift.'

'He told me.'

She went to one of the tall windows, which Pietro unlocked so that she could stand outside on the balcony.

'The bride and groom would have come to stand here together,' Pietro told her, 'and everyone in the gondolas going past would have hailed them. Did he tell you that?'

'Probably. He said so many things. I suppose he believed them when he said them. But I don't think that wedding was ever going to happen. More and more the whole thing feels like a book I read about someone else.'

'How much do you mind?'

'I'll tell you that when I know how it ends—if it ever ends.'

'Do you often think that way?' he asked.

'I think it more and more. Have you heard anything from Gino?'

'No. I can't contact him.'

'Which means he doesn't want to talk to you. Or rather, he doesn't want to talk to me. Ah well.'

She stood looking up at the full moon, covering the scene with silver.

'I wonder if it's going to rain,' she said.

'Yes, it is,' he said as a drop fell on him. 'I think the storm is approaching with a vengeance. Let's get inside.'

He locked the window and they left the

ballroom, climbing the stairs to his apartment. Toni was there, lying on the floor, and he came towards them as he always did. But he didn't stay long tonight, seeming anxious to get back to his shabby sofa and curl up again.

Ruth wasn't sure what made her kneel down beside him, suddenly disturbed.

'What is it, old boy?' she whispered. 'Are you all right?'

But he wasn't, and the next minute Toni made a convulsive movement, gave a huge gasp, as if choking, and began to shake violently.

'Poor old boy,' Ruth said at once. 'You're having a seizure, aren't you? Here, come on.'

She reached out and tried to put her arms about the big body that was thrashing madly in a way that might have been alarming if she hadn't seen this before. She murmured soothingly, knowing the poor creature could hear very little, but trying to get through to him with a wordless message of comfort.

'It won't last long,' Pietro said. 'Just a few minutes. Shall I take him? When he starts thrashing around he gets a bit violent.'

'No, leave him with me,' Ruth said. 'I don't mind what he does.'

Even as she spoke Toni's teeth sank into her wrist. She winced and pulled herself free.

'He didn't mean that,' Pietro said quickly. 'He doesn't know what he's doing.'

'Of course he doesn't,' she said, taking the dog in her arms again. 'It's not his fault. Is there anything special that you normally do for him when he has fits?'

'No, just hold him and wait for it to pass.'

'Then he just needs to know that he's loved and protected, and he'll come through it.' She turned back to Toni. 'Come on, my love. Hold on to me, and we'll see it through together. There, then—it's all right—it's going to be all right, my darling.'

At first he didn't seem to hear, but gradually the thrashing quietened, and Toni lay in her arms, still shaking, but calmer as Ruth stroked his head and kissed his shaggy fur.

'There, my love,' she whispered. 'I'm here—I'm here. There's nothing to worry about.'

She continued to soothe him, unaware that Pietro was watching her with a startled look in his eyes. A man who'd stumbled on buried treasure and feared to believe what he'd discovered might have looked like that. But Ruth didn't see it.

'Has he hurt you?' Pietro asked at last, sounding oddly husky.

'No, he didn't break the skin,' she said, looking at her wrist. 'He didn't mean it, did you, darling?'

'He's an Italian dog,' Pietro reminded her. 'If you talk in English he doesn't understand.'

'Of course he understands. It's not the words, it's the tone of voice. He knows I'm on his side, and I love him.' She kissed Toni's head again, murmuring, 'You know I love you, don't you?'

'Then I guess if he knows that—he knows everything,' Pietro said slowly.

He rose and backed away, his eyes fixed on the two on the sofa, enfolded together, content to be so. Toni's eyes were closed and his breathing became more regular as he relaxed, trusting Ruth completely. Pietro waited for her to look up, but all her attention was for the vulnerable creature in her arms.

It was a novel experience for Pietro to be ignored, and he gave a wry smile at himself as he made the supper. Ruth left the sleeping Toni, while she went to the table for the shortest possible time, and ate without taking her eyes from the dog. Afterwards she returned to the sofa and sat beside the dog, stroking his head.

'Don't you want to go to bed?' Pietro asked.

'No, I'm staying with him. He needs to feel safe. And we're special friends.'

'He certainly seems to think so. He isn't usually so peaceful after a seizure. I'm afraid, after this, he's not going to be satisfied with just me.'

'Yes, he will. In his world you're "the one". I'm

just passing through. When I'm gone, you'll still be his rock.'

'When you're gone,' he murmured.

They were quiet for a while.

'Listen to that noise,' she said, turning her head to the window. 'It must be raining in torrents.'

'Well, you know plenty about storms in Venice.'

She smiled suddenly and said in a teasing voice, 'I wonder if there's anyone standing out there, looking like a drowned rat.'

'Want me to take a look?'

'No, if she's there, best leave her. She'll only be trouble, and you know about *that.*'

'The last one wasn't so bad,' Pietro said lightly.

'Really? I heard she was grumpy and awkward.'

'Definitely. Sharp-tongued, difficult and just plain contrary.'

'The sort you could well do without?' she urged.

'I thought so at first, but she grew on me. Plus my dog likes her, and that goes a long way with me.'

They laughed together. Toni stirred, grunting, and she soothed him. After a while she leaned back and closed her eyes, still holding him protectively. She dozed on and off for the rest of the night, and whenever she opened her eyes Pietro was there, watching her with an expression she didn't understand.

At dawn they were awoken by a nightmarish

sound that lasted for ten seconds, stopped for ten, then blared again for ten.

'That's the sirens,' Pietro said. 'High tide's on its way, and it's going to be a big one.'

Within seconds Minna and Celia were with them, running down the back stairs to start putting sandbags against the doors, to the accompaniment of the hideous squalling.

'I know,' Pietro said as Ruth put her hands over her ears. 'But it'll wake everyone in Venice, and that's the idea.'

Before they left home he told Minna what had happened to Toni, and she promised to watch him carefully.

'He won't have another fit because he never has them two days in succession,' he told Ruth as they walked away. 'But he'll be happier if they look in and talk to him.'

Aqua alta was clearly coming in, although it had only just begun to inch over the stone banks of the Grand Canal. When they reached St Mark's the water had risen to eight inches and the boards were in place so that they could walk over it.

Ruth was struck by the calm cheerfulness of the Venetians. To them this was a normal, if unwelcome, part of life. The shops around the piazza were built several steps up from the ground and, for the moment, the water had not reached them.

'But it soon will,' Pietro predicted.

'Do we put sandbags against the shop door?' she asked.

'Certainly not. If we blocked the door how would our customers get in?'

'Of course,' she mused. 'Why didn't I think of that?'

Mario was already at work, bringing out boards that he set up just above the water so that customers could come in and shop as normal. Now Ruth began to understand that the place had been designed with this in mind. Display cabinets were on high stilts, electric plugs were set halfway up the walls. For Venetians this was just how things were.

Trade was down that day, but not as much as she would have expected. When she expressed surprise her two companions laughed at her.

'That's the English for you, Mario,' Pietro said. 'One little drop of rain and they collapse.'

'One little—?' Ruth began to say, aghast. But then she joined in their laughter.

To her relief Pietro closed early and they splashed their way home. As Mario had warned her, it was hard to keep balance on the boards.

'The trouble is, everyone's going home at the same time,' Pietro said. 'Hold on to me.'

But he was too late. Somebody cannoned into her from behind, and the next moment she was in the water, lying flat on her back. Pietro was immediately beside her, hauling her to her feet, leaving them both soaked to the skin.

'The sooner we're home, the better,' he said, putting an arm firmly around her waist.

'I don't think we can get back on that board,' she said. 'It's too crowded.'

'Then we'll wade home. It's not far. Come on. Hold on to me.'

Clinging to each other, they splashed through the foot-high water until they reached the Riva del Ferro, which ran alongside the Grand Canal, and finally the side door of the palazzo.

'How are we going to get inside?' she cried. 'As soon as we open the door the water will pour in.'

'We're not going to open the door,' he said. 'I told you, we're prepared.'

Taking a key from his pocket, he reached up and opened a window on the ground floor, about four feet from the ground.

'You first,' he said, lifting her in his arms so that she could climb in, but she fell clumsily, landing on one knee and crying, 'Ouch!'

He followed at once, locking the window behind him, and shivering.

'Are you all right?'

'Yes, I just banged my knee. You go on up ahead.' She limped to the bottom of the stairs.

'There's no time for that,' he said, lifting her bodily. 'Just let's get in the warm.'

Holding her high against his chest, he made the stairs in double quick time.

'How come I keep getting soaked?' she demanded. 'I've barely been here three weeks and this is the second time.'

'Maybe Fate's trying to tell you something,' he suggested.

'Like "grow fins"?'

'You can have the first shower,' he said, setting her down in the apartment and fending off the dog, who tried to trip them up in his eagerness.

'Thanks. Hallo, Toni, have you been all right? Oh, yes, you look better.'

'Can you walk?'

'Yes, it was just a little knock. I'll be fine when I'm warm.'

It was bliss to get under the hot water. She would have lingered except that she didn't want him to freeze waiting for her. In a few minutes she was out, wrapped in a bath robe.

'It's all yours,' she told him.

But instead of dashing straight in he frowned, looking at her knee, where a mark showed clearly.

'You're going to have a nasty bruise there,' he said. 'Let me look.'

Sitting her down on the sofa, he dropped down

before her, and examined the injury, which was turning an ugly red.

'I should have climbed in the window first and helped you in,' he groaned.

'Will you stop blaming yourself? It was an accident. Nobody's fault. Go into the bathroom and get dry.'

'No, let me—'

'Pietro, please go,' she said in a suddenly strained voice. 'I don't want your pneumonia on my conscience.'

'But that should be looked at—'

'Go,' she said fiercely. 'I have to get dry.'

He rose quickly, almost snatching his hands from her skin. When he'd gone Ruth crossed her arms over her chest, trying to blank out the awareness of him that had gone through her like lightning, taking her totally by surprise. It had been the briefest possible moment, but it had been enough to show her the intimacy of their life in a new light.

Friends. Brother and sister. She'd asked for no more. But his touch had reminded her that she was naked beneath the towel robe. There had been a flash of excitement, an insidious sweetness that threatened her before she could control it.

But she was in control now, she assured herself. And life had enough complications without adding another.

Suddenly she didn't want to talk to Pietro again that evening. She wasn't sure why, but it had something to do with the memory that had nearly come to her a few days ago when she'd been talking to Mario.

'Venetian dialect,' she murmured now. 'We were saying—something about—what was it? And why does it trouble me now, even though I don't know what it is? *Why can't I remember?'*

Because you're afraid to remember, warned a voice in her head. Because once you've remembered nothing will ever be the same again. And you're not sure you're ready for that.

CHAPTER SEVEN

RUTH couldn't face an evening in Pietro's company. If he noticed her agitation he might guess the reason, and that would be worse than anything. Calling through the bathroom door, she told him that she needed an early night and was going straight to bed. By the time he emerged she had gone.

She lay awake for a long time, wishing her seething brain would grow calmer, but she was still restless when she finally fell asleep. And in that uneasy state, the memory she'd been seeking came back to her.

It was happening again; she was clasping him, whispering *'Te voja ben'*, kissing him again and again. But it wasn't Gino in her arms, not Gino's mouth she had kissed with such passion.

'Lie back, you're safe now.'

When she'd heard his voice she'd known it was true. She was safe. She had opened her eyes and seen Pietro.

No, she thought in urgent self-defence. She could not have kissed Pietro and not known it.

But his mouth was a different shape from Gino's, wider, stronger, more mobile. She felt it now against her own as surely as if he were there with her, and she knew which man she had kissed.

Shocked, she opened her eyes. It was still there, real, sharp-edged, horrifying. It had been Pietro all the time.

Not by a word or a look had he given her a sign in the days since. He understood, of course. He hadn't blamed her, had refused to embarrass her. But it had happened, and she couldn't escape it.

And now, appalled, she remembered something else. When he had first brought her in from the storm he had undressed her completely, holding her naked body in his arms after he stripped off her wet clothes, then replaced them with dry ones.

He had done it as impersonally as a nurse. She trusted him well enough to believe that. And yet as she thought of it heat began to spread through her body. He seemed to be there with her, holding her steady while she kissed him frantically with kisses that were meant for Gino, and vowed her love again and again.

She groaned, dropping her head into her hands, wondering how she could ever face him again.

'He must never know that I've realised,' she

whispered. 'I'd die of shame. I will never, *never* let him guess.'

It was easy to say, harder to do. When she went out next morning Minna was already there, pouring coffee, which was a relief as it would surely make things easier. But then Pietro smiled at her, and his mouth was the one she had pressed to hers in her delirium. For a shocking moment she could feel the firm shape of it. And then she knew that nothing was going to be easy.

'It's not like you to sleep late,' he chided her good humouredly.

'I didn't get much sleep last night. I think I'd rather stay here today if you can manage without me.'

Something uneasy in her voice made him come to stand in front of her and put his hands on her shoulders, saying gently, 'What is it, Ruth? Aren't you well?'

'I'm fine, I'm fine,' she said quickly.

'You don't sound fine. Has something happened to upset you?'

'No, of course not,' she said, wishing he wouldn't stand so close.

'You'd tell me if it had, wouldn't you?'

'Pietro, I'm telling you it's nothing. I just didn't sleep, that's all.'

If only he would remove his hands from her

shoulders, she thought desperately. Didn't he realise that his nearness now caused a fierce reaction to flow through her that she didn't know how to handle?

But of course he didn't know. And he must never know.

Having reached its peak, *aqua alta* began to recede. Within a day the level was normal and the Venetians began the all-too-familiar job of erasing it from their city.

Ruth helped Mario sweep the last of the water out of the shop, and soon nobody would have known that anything was wrong. It was a point of pride to recover as soon as possible, refusing to let the crisis make a difference.

But there were some for whom this wasn't possible. Late that afternoon the door of the shop was flung open and Barone Franco came flying in as fast as his bulk would allow. He was almost in tears.

'Disaster!' he cried. 'A terrible tragedy. Where is my friend Pietro?'

'Right here,' Pietro soothed him. 'Whatever has happened, Franco?'

'My palace is ruined, destroyed.'

Pietro calmed him down and managed to draw out the details. It transpired that the house on the island had suffered grievously from the high tide. While not actually ruined, it was in no state for the glamorous ball that was planned, and for which so many expensive tickets had been sold.

'Franco, I warned you that you didn't protect that place properly,' Pietro said gently. 'When you did it up you skimped on the safety features.'

'There was no time. It would have taken several more months. Serafina set her heart on this ball. Now it's a mess. There's only a few days to go, and there's no time to put it right. Serafina is devastated. I must find somewhere else, but everywhere suitable is already taken for other things. Pietro, my friend—'

'No,' Pietro said at once. 'Forget it, Franco.'

'But who else can I ask? Pietro, I beg you—you have that great building standing empty. You wouldn't have to do anything. My own people will come in and get it ready. You won't be troubled.'

Looking at Pietro's face, Ruth could tell that this was far from the truth. The thought of strangers invading his peaceful home was horrible to him. But Franco couldn't see this. He continued pestering while Pietro listened, a withered expression on his face and his hand clenching and unclenching out of sight. Only Ruth noticed this and it gave her a strange feeling, as though the two of them were apart from the rest of the world.

'The trouble with you,' Franco burbled, 'is that it's been too long since you enjoyed yourself. You ought to get out more, give a party.'

'I'm sorry, but I can't agree—'

'Of course you can. It's not good to shut yourself away. You don't really mean to refuse me.'

Ruth regarded the insensitive oaf with something close to hate. She was consumed by a fierce protectiveness towards Pietro. His wealth, his grand status were suddenly nothing, and all she could see was how alone he was. She wanted to scream at Franco, For pity's sake shut up! Can't you see what you're doing to him?

But she stayed silent, knowing that, in his defiant solitude, Pietro would resent any attempt to rescue him.

Franco burbled on, oblivious. 'You've hidden away too long. Now it's time to snap out of it. Lisetta wouldn't have wanted you to grieve for ever, and this will be the perfect way to come back to the world. Besides, think of having to send back all the tickets.'

'You're quite right,' Pietro said in a tight voice. 'By all means let us have the ball in the Palazzo Bagnelli. How shrewd of you to appeal to the businessman in me.'

Franco beamed, taking this at its face value. But that wasn't the reason, Ruth knew. Pietro had given in because he was on the rack, and it was the only way to make Franco shut up.

'I knew you'd see sense,' he chortled. 'Why don't we go back there now and—?'

'Tomorrow would be better,' Pietro said quietly.

'But I'm here now. Let's get going.'

Pietro's hand clenched on a piece of decorative wood and his voice was very controlled, alarmingly controlled, Franco would have thought if he were more perceptive.

'We will discuss this tomorrow,' he repeated.

Still the bumbling fool wouldn't understand. 'But there's so much to settle. Come on, we'll have a bottle of wine and—'

He stopped. Franco had raised his head and looked him in the eyes. Ruth thought she would have died if he'd turned that look on her. There was more in it than resentment. There was sheer murderous hate for this creature who stomped all over his most sacred memories with hobnailed boots.

At last Franco understood. He faltered into silence, grew pale, and even stepped back as though afraid that Pietro might strike him. But that wouldn't happen, Ruth knew. Pietro had no need of his fists when his eyes could convey such a terrifying message.

'I'll see you tomorrow,' Pietro said quietly, and

walked out of the shop, across St Mark's and into the labyrinth of *calles*.

He went on walking for an hour, caring nothing for where he went, seeing nothing, feeling nothing except the inner emptiness that was his defence against a feeling that was a thousand times worse. When he became aware of his surroundings he found he was approaching his home.

He moved mechanically, going to his room, switching on the computer, reading it with dead eyes, checking his emails.

And there was one from Gino.

Ruth arrived later that evening, having resisted the temptation to hurry after Pietro. He wouldn't thank her for dogging his footsteps, she knew.

Her resolutions were all made. The earthquake that had happened inside her was something he must never be allowed to suspect, and until she was more sure of herself she would keep her distance.

There was no sign of him when she entered, but she could hear his steps coming from behind the closed door of his room. This way, then that, then back again, like a prisoner pacing his cell. Once she thought she heard a fist being slammed down. Then there was silence again while she stood, wondering what to do.

Without warning the door opened.

'Don't stand there,' he said curtly. 'I've been waiting for you to come in.'

'I didn't want to disturb you.'

'Thanks, but a pot of strong English tea would do me more good.'

She made some and took a large mug of tea in to him.

'Where's yours?' he wanted to know. 'I hate drinking alone.'

When she returned he said, 'I sent Minna to bed, so I'm afraid it's make-do-and-mend in the kitchen.'

'I had something on the way home.'

'Are you being tactful?' he demanded suspiciously.

'I thought it might make a nice contrast to Franco.'

He groaned and spooned sugar into his mug. He'd taken a fancy to the tea she made, and would sometimes drink it in preference to coffee.

Ruth was feeling her way carefully. The resolve to keep her distance had died with the first sight of his haggard face. The protectiveness she'd felt in the shop came surging back.

'This is Franco's fault,' she said angrily. 'Why did you say he could bring his party here? You could have simply thrown him out.'

'Could I?' Pietro said ironically. 'Do you think that would have stopped him? It wouldn't. He'd have ground on and on until I'd have had to kill him to make him shut up.'

'Killing him might have been a good idea,' she said thoughtfully.

Pietro shook his head. 'Bad for business.'

'I suppose.'

'I was becoming afraid of what I might do. So I said yes.'

'But that didn't really shut him up.' She sighed. 'He just found something else to badger you about—until you gave him that look.'

'You saw it, then?'

'Oh, yes.'

'Did it give much away?' he asked, apparently indifferent.

'Plenty.'

'He'll never know what danger he was in at that moment.'

'Oh, I think he knows,' she said lightly. 'He got a grandstand view of your eyes.'

Pietro gave a grunt that might have been satisfaction.

'Anyway, it's too late now,' he said. 'I've agreed and I won't go back on my word, but I'd give anything not to have this happen.'

He saw her looking at him and grimaced.

'I know, I know. I sound like a mean, miserable old miser, turning his back on the world.'

'You're not old,' she said, venturing to tease him a little.

He gave a faint smile. 'Thanks.'

'And why shouldn't you turn your back on the world if that's what you want to do?'

'It's commonly held to be a bad thing.'

'But if the world no longer has anything that you want, why should you pretend about it? What's the point of being a count if you can't get your own way?'

'I wish my father could hear you. He was an aristocrat of the old-fashioned type. If you had a title then certain things were expected of you. It was your duty to present a particular face to the world and behave in a lordly manner, no matter how you felt inside. Plus, of course, you always got your own way.'

'But you don't agree?'

'His beliefs were right for his time, but not for now.'

'Then you don't have to go on with this. There must be someone else's place Franco can take over. Don't just give in to him.'

'You're very fierce. I wouldn't like to meet you in a *calle* on a dark night, in this mood. Perhaps I should warn Franco.'

'I'm only saying you should keep your home the way you want it.'

'The way I want it,' he sighed.

She could have kicked herself. Of course this desolation wasn't the home he wanted. Without the woman he loved it was simply all he had left.

The woman he loved. She'd always known it with her head, but now she realised what it really meant. It meant that he'd chosen to die inside rather than live without her. Somewhere inside Ruth there was an ache.

'I shouldn't have said that,' she said awkwardly. 'It's none of my business—about your wife. I'm sorry.'

He became suddenly still, as though she'd struck him. Slowly he turned and gave her a keen look.

'What do you know about my wife?' he asked in a strange voice.

When Ruth didn't answer, Pietro said, 'What is it, Ruth? What did you mean about my wife?'

'Nothing. I had no right to mention her. I didn't want to make you angry.'

'I'm not angry, but I would like you to answer me. Just how much do you know about her?'

He sounded as if he resented her knowing anything, Ruth thought, her heart sinking. Had his love really been so powerfully possessive that even the mention of her name was forbidden to others?

'I know hardly anything,' she said awkwardly. 'Just that she died last year, and it hit you very hard. It must have done for you to turn away from the world like this.'

'Like I said, mean, miserable miser,' he replied ironically.

'That's your business. You don't have to grieve the way other people think you should. Only you know what—' She forced herself to stop, afraid of making everything worse.

'Yes, only I know,' he said quietly.

'No, that's not true,' she said, gathering her courage. 'She must have known as well.'

'Known what?' He turned quickly to look at her, and there was a strange, keen look in his eyes.

'How dreadfully you loved her. She must have known that. People don't just understand what we say, but what they feel in the atmosphere.'

'So you don't think the words matter very much?'

'Yes, the words are nice, but they're not everything.'

'I thought women attached a lot of importance to them.'

'That's because we know a lot of men don't find them easy. So if he manages them, it means more. But if he doesn't—I promise you a woman knows the man who loves her and the man who doesn't. Whether he says it or not, it's there in the tone of his voice, the way his eyes rest on her, the things he remembers to do.'

She had meant to comfort him with the thought that his wife had died content in the knowledge of his love, but to her horror he closed his eyes suddenly and turned his head away. She groaned, realising how insensitive she had been.

'I'm sorry, I'm sorry,' she said hurriedly. 'Please forget I said anything. What do I know?'

'Don't put yourself down,' he said, turning back. 'I think I'd rely on your experience more than anyone's.'

'Even when I can't remember what it was?' she asked wryly.

'Especially then.'

'That doesn't make any sense.'

'It makes perfect sense. If you're not using your memory you're relying on your instincts. I trust your instincts.'

'Thank you,' she said softly. 'I wish there was some way I could help you. But nothing really helps, does it?'

'I once believed that. I've sat in this place and listened to the silence and wondered how I was going to get through the rest of my life. I'm not sure how I'd cope if I had your problems, probably not as well as you do, but I can talk to you, not to anyone else.'

'But you don't— I mean, we never talk about

anything much, unless it's about me,' Ruth protested. 'You don't talk about you.'

'But you were the one who said the words mattered less than what you pick up in the atmosphere.' He gave a brief laugh. 'You might describe our atmosphere as two desperate characters drowning. But we're not drowning anymore.'

'Not as long as we just cling on to each other,' she said. 'You're right. It makes all the difference.'

'With any luck we may hold each other up until one of us can touch the bottom,' he said lightly.

'One of us? If I can touch land do you think I'm going to go off and leave you to drown?' she asked. 'Would you leave me?'

He shook his head.

'That's what I thought,' she said softly.

Ruth fetched him another mug of tea and when she returned he was going through a large photo album. Several more rested on a chair.

'I gathered these to get them out of Franco's way when he takes over the building,' he said.

To her surprise she saw the pictures were of children; two boys and a girl. The boys were in their late teens, the girl about thirteen.

'That's me,' Pietro said, pointing. 'The other one was my friend Silvio, and the girl was Lisetta, his sister. She used to trail along behind us, and we were kind to her in that selfish, casual way of boys.'

'What are you doing?' Ruth asked, peering closer. 'You all look as though you're about to throw something.'

'Dice. We had a special game where you had to toss the dice better than anyone else. If you won, the prize was a stone. Lisetta played it better than either of us. She had a naturally straight "eye". She'd win stone after stone, and when she had a pile of stones, she'd risk the whole lot on one throw. Sometimes she won, more often she lost, but losing never bothered her. She'd just laugh and start again.'

He studied the picture, smiling. 'I think it was her idea of being kind—let the boys win in the end so that they don't feel too bad.'

'That sounds very traditional. Was she really like that?'

'She was very kind.'

'Is this her?' Ruth had come across a large portrait of the same girl, now grown up, dressed in the garb of a college graduate.

'That's her on the day she graduated with honours,' Pietro said. 'She was the bright one, put us all to shame. After that she became a professor herself, the youngest they'd ever had.'

'Wow!'

Ruth studied the calm face, which already held more than a touch of assurance. She wasn't pretty, but she was handsome, and she looked as though she did nothing by chance.

Something made her look back to the first picture. There were several of them showing her ready to throw the dice, always smiling, and always with something in her eyes that made Ruth sure Pietro had misread her.

This wasn't an old-fashioned girl letting the boys win out of a misplaced concern for male pride. This was a high roller with the nerve to stake her entire winnings on one throw, and the courage to laugh if she lost. Even as a child it had been there. Later, beneath the professor's exterior, beat the heart of a risk-taker. Ruth found herself liking Lisetta.

For her wedding she'd worn a fancy confection of satin and lace that didn't quite fit with the severity of her looks. Her veil swept the ground, her bouquet was enormous, but what stood out most was the look of blazing happiness on her face. There could be no mistaking her feelings, even when she was pictured alone. But when she was looking into Pietro's smiling face she was consumed by radiant joy.

Until now Ruth had pitied him, grieving for the woman he'd loved, but this was also the woman who had given him an adoration few men ever knew. What would it do to him to lose that love?

Looking around at the bleakness of his life, Ruth thought she knew.

She found him watching her. Without a word he took the photo and put it out of sight.

'She looks like a marvellous person,' she ventured.

'She was, generous and giving…' His voice trailed away and he sat staring at the floor, his hands clasped between his knees.

She could bear his pain no longer. Dropping to the floor, she laid her hands over his.

'If only there was something I could say,' she whispered.

He shook his head. 'You don't need to. If I could talk to anyone, it would be to you, but— Ruth, I wanted to say…I wish things were different. I wish I was any use with words—'

She silenced him with her fingertips over his mouth. Then, because it seemed natural, she slipped her arms around him. He hugged her back with all the force of a man who hadn't been hugged for a long time, and they held each other in silence for a while.

CHAPTER EIGHT

RUTH waited, tense with hope to see if Pietro would move his hands over her, but he only held her without stirring until at last he disengaged himself. Now he would send her away, she thought, but he got to his feet, saying, 'I need a walk before I can sleep. If we're keeping an eye on each other, are you coming?'

'Yes, of course.'

As they reached the door downstairs they heard a soft pattering of feet and Toni caught up with them.

'I guess we're all going,' Ruth said.

'He never did like being left behind.'

Pietro locked the door behind them, then crooked his arm for her to slip her hand through it, and they began to wander through the tiny streets, lit only by a faint silver glow from above. At first they did not speak, and for a while the only sound was their feet echoing on the paving stones, and the soft noise of Toni padding behind them.

'I think this must be the quietest place on earth,' Ruth mused. 'Anywhere else you'd always be able to hear a car, even at night, but here there's no noise at all.'

'Oh, yes, there's noise, if you know how to hear it,' Pietro said. 'Listen to the water.'

She listened, and understood what he meant. From every direction came the plash of water on stone, so soft that it was almost part of the silence, yet unmistakably there.

She was content, almost happy. The disturbing feeling towards Pietro that was growing inside her could be set aside for the moment, while she relished their camaraderie. Somehow she knew that her previous life had never been blessed with anything like this.

They strolled on peacefully, keeping to the narrowest backstreets. Outwardly Pietro was as calm as she, but inwardly he was troubled.

I should have told her by now, but how shall I say it?

'Let's go this way,' she said, drawing him sideways.

'Do you know what lies this way?' he asked curiously.

'A tiny canal, and a tiny bridge. I like them better than the big, glamorous places.'

'So do I.'

There were a hundred tiny canals and tiny bridges, but he knew the one she meant, and after a while they came to it and went to stand on the bridge, looking down into the depths. Here and there a light was still on in one of the buildings, the reflection dancing in the ripples on the water.

From somewhere came the sound of a horn as a ship began its journey out of the lagoon, away to foreign parts, sending waves running back through the large canals, then the small ones, so that even here the water danced higher before settling back.

Another long, contented silence. Then came the sound that sent a pleasurable shiver down Ruth's spine, a yodelling wail, coming out of the darkness, echoing from wall to wall before dying away into the distance. A pause, then it came again, finally shivering into silence.

'Do you know what that is?' Pietro asked.

'Yes, it's a gondolier, signalling that he's coming around a blind corner,' she said. 'There he is.'

As they watched a long shape drifted into sight, turning towards them, the gondolier plying his oar at the rear, in front of him a young man and woman in each other's arms.

I must tell her now, Pietro thought.

Down below the lovers looked up, then smiled

and waved, as though wanting to share their happiness with the world, before vanishing under the bridge.

I will tell her, but how will she take it?

The email from Gino had said,

I know you think I should have returned before, but I've been doing so well in Poland, finding all sorts of new places that will interest you. I'd planned to go on to Russia next—after all, that was what you originally told me to do—but it will mean being away for a long time and I suppose I ought to clear this other thing up first, otherwise it'll just drag on.

I'm coming by train from Milan, and I'll be at the station the day after tomorrow, at about five-thirty in the afternoon. If it's all right with you I'll stay the night, and leave the next day. That'll give me time to talk to Ruth and put her right about whatever's worrying her.

Pietro had read this several times, trying vainly to detect any hint of concern for the girl Gino had once loved and planned to marry. But it was a fruitless task, and at last he had begun to outline a reply. As he had tapped out the letters his face had been concentrated into a scowl.

Whatever you're planning to say I can't imagine that it will do Ruth any good. She puts a brave face on it, but she's having a hard time and I don't want you to make it worse. It's best if you don't come at all. Ruth is no longer your problem. I'll take care of her.

Then he sat glaring at the computer screen, struggling with the biggest temptation of his life. But at last he gave in with a bad grace, and hit the Delete button so savagely that the keyboard jumped.

He tried again.

Don't come at all if that's your attitude. She's better off without you.

He deleted that one at once and scowled at the screen, trying to understand what was wrong with him. With all his heart he wanted to keep Gino away and save Ruth from pain and disillusion.

But he couldn't save her. It was her decision. He could neither shield her, nor make it for her. That was the brute fact that he couldn't get past.

As for why he should want to intervene, that was another fact, an alarming one, that he didn't want to face.

He'd been living in a spell, telling himself that

it could never be broken, that tomorrow wouldn't come. Now it had come and he was left in confusion.

'Did Gino take you in a gondola?' he asked.

'Several times. He actually proposed to me in a gondola.'

Suppressing the bitter comment, 'He would!', Pietro said noncommittally, 'Tell me about it.'

He couldn't make out her face very clearly, but well enough to discern the change of expression: a quick smile, followed at once by a reflective look, then another smile, different, softer, full of sweet recollection. It hurt him to see it.

'I can't,' she said at last.

'You don't remember the details?'

'No, I can remember them but I can't—talk about them.'

He wanted to lash out. Clearly, to her, the events of that night were too sacred to be mentioned, but Gino had merely talked of clearing up 'this other thing'.

This other thing. How could Ruth ever imagine that her lover would speak of her like that? And when she found out, how could he prevent it destroying her?

'Do you think you could cope with seeing Gino again?' he asked quietly.

'That's not likely to happen anytime soon.'

'It might happen sooner than you think.' He took a deep breath. 'I've heard from him.'

She turned quickly. 'What did he say?'

'He's coming home.'

He wished he could read her face. Were her eyes wide with shock or joyous disbelief?

'Is that really true?' she whispered. 'He called you?'

'He emailed me. His train from Milan will get into the station the day after tomorrow, at about five-thirty in the afternoon.'

'Why didn't you tell me before?'

'I wasn't sure how. Things are different now. You've moved on.'

'Not—' she started to say, then quickly checked herself.

What had she meant to say? he wondered. Not really? Not that much?

'I don't know,' she finished at last. 'I just don't know.'

From a few feet away came a faint whine. Toni had left the bridge and gone to the entrance to a narrow *calle*, where he sat, impatient to go home.

'All right,' she laughed. 'We're coming.'

Pietro sighed at the way Toni had dispelled the mood. Another few minutes and he might have drawn Ruth out about her true feelings, but the dog's interruption had given her the chance to think and settle her defences in place.

'Next time I'll leave you behind,' he threatened his faithful hound.

'Don't be unkind to him,' Ruth said firmly. 'Come on, pet, I'll give you your medicine as soon as we get indoors.'

The moment had gone.

As they wandered home Pietro said, 'I wish you wouldn't shut me out.'

'I'm not,' she insisted. 'Not deliberately, anyway. In an odd way, I'm shut out too—shut out from myself. There's somebody in there called "Me", but she won't open the door to—me. Does that make any sense?'

'Oddly enough, it does. Go on.'

'How am I going to react to seeing Gino? The point is, which one of me will do the reacting?' She gave a little laugh. 'Maybe it'll be like one of those horror films when one person vanishes into another. One look at Gino and Ruth One will appear and take over.'

'She's the one who's in love with him.'

'*Was* in love with him. She's gone, but—'

Pietro nodded. 'But how far?'

'Or maybe Ruth Three will stand there, resolute, and say "I'm in charge now,"' she said, avoiding a direct answer. 'And he'll run for his life.'

He looked at her, walking beside him, poised, elegant and beautiful.

'I don't think he'll run for his life,' he said. 'More likely he'll try to win you back.'

'That could be awkward, two of us operating in different time zones,' she said lightly.

'What about Ruth Two?'

'Perish the thought. I don't want to be her again. Now, I'm not going to think about it until I go to the station and meet the train.'

'Until *we* go,' Pietro said firmly.

'I'll be all right on my own.'

'I'm going to be there. Don't argue with me.'

'All right. You said Gino emailed you. Can I see it?'

'I'm afraid I deleted it by accident.'

Her smile had never been more brilliant. 'I see. All right, Toni, I'm coming.'

She skipped ahead, leaving him to trail after her, dissatisfied.

Next day Franco came to the Palazzo Bagnelli, bringing his wife. Ruth found the Baronessa Serafina pure entertainment. Born Jessie Franks, she had changed her name to Sweetheart for a brief career as an adult movie star, and then again to Serafina in honour of her new, grand position in the world. But only Franco was permitted to call her this. To everyone else she was Baronessa, and woe betide anyone who forgot.

Her manner to Pietro combined awe and flirtatiousness, neither of which appealed to him, Ruth could see. She made it plain that she considered herself, her husband and Count Bagnelli to exist on a higher plane than mere mortals. Ruth was relegated to the position of servant, or would have been if Pietro hadn't made a point of treating her with noticeable respect.

'If I'd known she was going to be so rude to you I'd never have agreed,' he said. 'Shall I throw them out?'

'Of course not. She doesn't bother me. I think she's hilarious, except when she insults the house.'

'Quite!' he seethed. 'Did you hear her say it needed redecoration?'

'It's not enough like a Hollywood mansion for her taste.'

The list of things Serafina wanted altered was enormous, and only a flat refusal from Pietro silenced her. Attempting to smooth things over, Franco insisted on taking them all to dinner. Serafina's eyebrows rose at the idea of including Ruth, but Ruth backed out thankfully, preferring an evening alone with Toni. Pietro wasn't pleased.

'How can you leave me undefended?' he growled to Ruth.

'Because I don't fancy being treated as Cinderella, allowed to go to the ball. She'd expect me to vanish at midnight.'

'Great. Then I could vanish with you.'

'Sorry. She's your problem.'

'Thanks!'

It was a relief to have the building to herself, and to hear the blessed quiet after the disturbance of the day. For tomorrow an army would descend on them and there would be no moments of calm.

Soon she would see Gino again, and discover whether the man who lived in her head had any reality. If he did, then the thing she feared most might happen, and she would be transported back to a discarded personality, becoming again the woman who was in love with him.

But she longed not to be that woman. The thought that it might happen was like seeing a cage close around her.

And yet another part of her heart yearned to feel again the innocent love and delight she had known then, when the world was a happier, simpler place.

She fell asleep hoping that tonight her dreams would give her some guidance, but this time there was only darkness.

Franco and Serafina descended again next morning, complete with servants to make the

Palazzo Bagnelli 'suitable', as they saw it. Pietro had taken the precaution of telephoning his country estate and summoning some of his own servants who had worked there before. They arrived like an opposing army, ready to take charge.

Arguments followed. Minna waded into battle, swearing vengeance on anyone who touched a vase or cleaned a tile without her express permission. Celia, armed and dangerous, stood at the door to the kitchen ready to repel invaders. But Franco's cook had a tact and charm that won her over, and peace was soon established.

'I left Celia showing the assistant cooks around the cupboards,' Pietro said to Minna in a quiet moment late that afternoon. 'Thank heavens that's settled.'

'But there's a great deal that isn't settled, signore,' Minna informed him, a martial light in her eye. 'Let me tell you—'

'It'll have to wait, I'm afraid. Time's getting on and I have to go out. Do you know where Ruth is?'

'She went out half an hour ago.'

'Out? Did she say where?'

'No, signore, but I saw her turn to cross the Rialto Bridge.'

Then she was heading for the railway station, Pietro realised. She'd said she would prefer to go alone, and she'd simply slipped away while he was occupied.

Franco appeared. 'Pietro, my friend—'

'Not now,' Pietro said hurriedly and headed for the door.

'But this is important.'

'So is this.'

He made his escape before Franco could stop him, running out of the house, over the Rialto Bridge, then plunging into the rabbit warren of *calles* that would lead him to the railway station on the extreme edge of Venice.

As he ran he cursed her: stupid woman, obstinate woman, he'd *told* her it was better if he came too. Why couldn't she see that?

But she'd never been sensible. After the first day when she'd been only half-alive, she'd done things her own way, no matter what he said, accepting as little of his protection as she could manage, and always ready to tease and infuriate him, to keep him at a careful distance.

And that was the clue to her state of mind. This meeting with Gino was more important than she let on, and when he thought of how many ways it could go wrong, his blood ran cold. He wished now that he'd warned her about Gino's attitude.

Or perhaps it didn't matter. Perhaps, with the first look, all trouble would be swept away. He'd find them locked in each other's arms, and that would be the end of that. He would go his way, she would go hers, with Gino, and it would be as though she had never come into his life.

She'd once warned him that she would soon be gone, but she'd been talking about Toni, and he hadn't understood the message.

Now the station was in sight. All he had to do was go in and search for her.

But something had happened to his limbs and he couldn't move.

There wasn't a train at exactly five-thirty but one was due ten minutes later, so Ruth settled herself to wait. It was vital to be sensible. Even if it went well, nothing was going to happen today. They probably wouldn't even recognise each other.

Yet her heart still beat with anticipation. Whatever the present might be, she had loved Gino passionately, and he was about to come back into her life.

Outside the station the world was dark. Ruth stood at the end of the platform watching the lights stream out over the two-mile causeway to the mainland, cars on one side, trains on the other. For the moment the line was empty.

But then a light began to move along it, heading for Venice, growing larger. Ruth's breath was coming so fast that she almost choked. She could see the train clearly now, details coming into view as it neared the station. She couldn't move.

As it came to a halt, doors were already opening. She searched the faces, looking for Gino's, but she couldn't see him. Suddenly she was desperate. How could she have overlooked him when his features were imprinted on her mind? People were beginning to stream past her. She raced to the other end of the platform so that he would have to pass her to leave the station.

Then it was all over. Everyone was gone, and none of them was Gino.

She stood still, pulling herself together, until she could force herself to move to the side where there was a seat. A man in the uniform of a railway employee asked if she was all right.

'That was the Milan train, wasn't it?' she asked.

'Oh, no, signorina. The Milan train is late today. It should be here in another ten minutes, on the next platform.'

The haze cleared. She was alive again.

She moved to the adjoining platform and, to give herself something to think of, concentrated on a poster advertising the coming carnival, due to start soon. For eleven days the revellers would dance, sing, eat too much, drink too much and indulge in whatever took their fancy. The last day of Carnival was the day before Ash Wednesday, and the pleasure would explode in a riot of extravagant jollity. Then Lent would begin, six weeks of abstinence and self-discipline.

'It's not too bad at first,' Gino had said. 'You start off so bloated with the things you enjoyed in Carnival that you're glad to have a rest from them. But then—' He'd shivered in mock horror.

Last year she'd seen only two days of festivities before it had been time to go home. For those days they had sung and danced and loved. And now it was Carnival again.

But he would be here at any moment. Already she could see the train in the distance, slowly approaching across the causeway. She positioned herself where she couldn't miss him and waited.

After a few moments the dread began to rise in her again. He wasn't here. She searched every face but not one of them was his.

But that wasn't possible. He had said he would be here. She began to run down the platform, desperately seeking the one man who could bring her nightmare to an end. Twice she reached out and stopped someone, but it wasn't Gino. People turned to stare at her, but she couldn't give up.

She had reached the end of the train. There was nothing to do but turn and go back, so she did, walking slowly as the full extent of the disaster dawned on her. Now she knew why Pietro had wanted to be with her. He'd known that something like this might happen, and he didn't want her to face it alone.

She stopped, with no energy to go further. All the defiant courage she had thrown against her troubles had come to nothing. She was no further forward than she had ever been, and she wanted to bang her head against the wall.

But then something made her look up and see the man standing watching her from a distance. He moved towards her and at the same moment she began to run, full of joy and relief, faster and faster until she could see his face clearly and know that it was the one face of all others that she needed at this moment.

He hadn't failed her. In her heart she had always known that he would be there. A cry broke from her as she ran into Pietro's arms and felt them close powerfully about her.

CHAPTER NINE

FOR a long time neither moved, just stood still, clasping each other, tightly. Ruth was possessed by a storm of relief. Pietro too was relieved, but also confused and troubled.

He heard her muffled exclamation of, 'Oh thank goodness! If you hadn't come I don't know what I'd have done.'

'Well, I'm here,' he said.

He spoke cautiously because he was afflicted by doubt. Did she know which man was holding her? Her joy as she rushed along the shadowy platform, the way she'd hurled herself at him, even her words, all these could have been for Gino as much as for himself. It was vital to know.

'Ruth,' he said, his mouth close to her hair. 'Ruth, look at me.'

'Give me a moment,' he heard in a muffled voice. 'I just want to hold you.'

But he could bear the tension no longer. 'No, look at me. You *must*.'

She raised her head, looking at him, and he searched her eyes, waiting for the moment of shock when she recognised him. But it didn't happen. She was smiling at the sight of his face.

She'd known it was him all the time. The relief was overwhelming.

'Thank you for coming,' she said. 'You were right.'

'Hasn't Gino arrived?' he asked gently.

'No, that was the Milan train, but he isn't on it. I suppose he changed his mind. You knew he would, didn't you?'

'I guessed it was possible. I just wanted to be here in case he did.'

'Isn't it time I stood on my own feet?' she asked shakily.

'Even someone standing on their own feet sometimes needs a hand to hold on to.'

From somewhere came the shrill sound of a cell phone. With a groan Pietro reached into his pocket and drew it out. Then he shouted, *'Gino.* Where the hell are you?'

'Look, I'm sorry,' came Gino's tinny voice. 'Something happened and I missed the train.'

'You amaze me,' Pietro said with loathing. 'So catch the next one.'

'That'll have to be tomorrow. Or perhaps the day after. I'll call you. Look, I'm really sorry—'

'Like hell you are! I think you should apologise o Ruth yourself.'

But Gino acted fast, so that Pietro heard him hang up before he could hand the phone to Ruth.

Pietro began to swear fiercely. Ruth listened with half her mind, trying to understand that Gino had backed out deliberately, leaving her still stranded in the desert. It was hard when she'd hought that time might be coming to an end. She ried to understand her own feelings but there was only dismay and emptiness.

'I'm going to murder him,' Pietro vowed.

'You'll have to find him first,' Ruth said with a wan little smile. 'I don't think that's going to be easy.'

'Ruth, I'm so sorry. If there was something I could do…'

'There is,' she said, going into his arms again. 'This is as good as a tonic.'

'Anytime you want.'

He drew her close in a bear hug and hid his face against her hair.

From nearby there was a shout. A cheerful man's voice yelled, 'There you are, folks! Wherever you ook, there are lovers. That's Venice for you!'

They ignored this, not realising that it related o them. But suddenly a crowd of young people was streaming around them, giving good-natured whistles.

'Oh, no!' Pietro groaned.

There were six youngsters, all in their late teens, wearing funny hats and out for a good time. One young man, just a little older and wearing a jester's cap, positioned himself to give a lecture, speaking English.

'A classic example of the species, ladies and gentlemen. He's come to meet her train, the train is late, they fly into each other's arms. Love triumphs, as always.'

'Beat it!' Pietro told him.

The jester was shocked.

'Sir, we are here in the spirit of Carnival. In fact, we *are* spirits of Carnival—'

'And I'll bet "spirits" is the right word,' Ruth declared, trying not to laugh.

'A small libation to while away the train journey,' the jester conceded. 'All right, two small libations, which have merely sharpened our intellect. Now we require only to see the completion of the process—'

'What completion?' Pietro demanded.

'A true love scene ends with a kiss. Only then can we be on our way, seeking new examples of *amore*.'

'Have them on me,' Pietro said, producing a

wad of notes and tossing them into the air where they were eagerly seized. 'Now be off.'

'But you haven't kissed the lady,' cried the jester, aghast.

The others took up the refrain, dancing around them, crying, 'Kiss, kiss!'

Pietro looked daggers, but Ruth could no longer contain her mirth. Watching her explode with laughter, feeling the vibration of her whole body against his, he felt her smile invade him, take him over, join him to her. The next moment he was joined to her in body as well as in spirit, his arm beneath her neck, his mouth on hers.

Ruth closed her eyes, not sure that this was happening, and only now understanding how much she'd wanted it to happen. The kiss she'd given him on the first night was still with her, reawakened now, a thousand times more intense.

She would have known his mouth of all others, no matter where or when. It was wide and firm, and it moved against hers with a combination of subtlety and power that was devastating. When she'd forced the first embrace on him he'd accepted it reluctantly, waiting until she was finished. But this was his kiss, coming fiercely from him to her, defying her not to return it.

It would have been beyond her power to resist the challenge, even if she'd wanted to. As it was, she was no longer stranded in a desert. Something within her was being set free, ready to soar.

Now she could submerge herself, knowing truly who was the man in her arms, wanting him there, trying to tell him so without words. When she felt his arms loosening about her she agreed, reluctantly, wanting to cling to him but knowing this wasn't the moment. But later, she promised herself.

Drawing away slightly, she saw his face as she'd never seen it before, full of a joy that matched her own, momentarily obliterating the world and all its problems. But there was something else too, a confusion that made him struggle and speak awkwardly.

'Well, we found a way to silence them,' he said.

'I hope so.' She looked around, ready to challenge their well-meaning tormentors.

They were alone.

'Where have they gone?' she said, baffled. 'Even the train's left.'

'I guess we took a little longer than we thought,' he said slowly.

'Ruth—'

'It's all right,' she said. 'Everything's all right.'

'Yes,' he agreed. 'Everything's all right.'

As they began the walk back along the platform to the exit he pondered, 'Ruth, did they really exist, or did we imagine them?'

A fantasy conjured out of the depths of their mutual need? It was a delightful thought, but she had to say, 'I think they were a crowd of English tourists who came for Carnival. And they're determined to see Carnival everywhere they look.'

'Well, at least we got rid of them.'

He spoke too soon. As they emerged from the great exit fronting the Grand Canal the tourists were waiting for them in a state of high glee.

'I said beat it,' Pietro groaned.

'But you haven't gone on to the next stage,' the jester said imploringly.

'The next stage?'

'The gondola ride, of course—gliding through the little darkened canals to the sound of a mandolin and a gondolier singing his heart out.'

'Thanks for the suggestion. I'll try to find one.'

'No need, we've hired everything necessary.'

Everyone gave elaborate bows, pointing the way to the water, where a gondola was waiting. On the rear platform stood a gondolier, and beside him stood a man with a mandolin, ready to serenade them. Also ready was a large motor boat, into which the tourists were already climbing.

'Oh, by the way,' the jester said placatingly, 'I said you'd be paying.'

By now the boatmen had recognised Pietro and were urgent in their apologies.

'All right, all right,' he growled. 'It's not your fault. I'll pay you, and we'll see this through to the end, otherwise they'll only have a bigger laugh.'

'And they say romance is dead!' the jester declared to his companions, who all cheered.

'I'm sorry about this,' he murmured to Ruth.

'Don't be. I'm enjoying it.'

In truth she was exhilarated. It was like being carried off by a runaway horse, not knowing where the horse was going, but sure she was going to be glad of it. She might have said a runaway gondola, but that couldn't describe the helter-skelter glee that was sweeping her up.

She wanted to cry up to the stars that she was ready to go on for ever.

Pietro climbed into the gondola first, and handed her in beside him. Before sitting he exchanged a few words in Venetian with the gondolier, who passed them on to the man driving the motor boat.

'What did you say?' Ruth demanded suspiciously.

'What do you think I said?'

'You probably told them to drown everyone.'

'No, I'm not as quick-witted as you. I didn't think of it in time.'

'So what did you say?'

'Stop nagging me, you little harpy.'

'I'm not little,' she said at once. 'I'm nearly as tall as you are. I'll show you.'

'Don't stand up in a gondola!'

'They're standing up.'

'They're used to it. You'll just capsize us.'

Since he had to seize her in his arms to restrain her this provoked more cheers from their audience.

'What did you say to them?' she repeated through her laughter.

'I'm not going to tell you,' he said defiantly. 'You'll just have to try to trust me.'

'Well, I don't trust you. You're hatching some terrible plan.'

He was in the spirit of it now, his eyes gleaming, partly with humour and partly with something else that made her catch her breath in joyous anticipation.

'You think you know me that well?' he challenged. 'I'm terrible?'

'Yes, you are. Absolutely terrible.'

The gondola rocked as they set out on their journey.

'So tell me what you said,' Ruth insisted.

'I forget.' He was teasing her now. She nudged him a little further.

'Tell me,' she urged.

'No. It's a secret.'

From behind them came a burst of laughter and the gondolier called, 'All is well, signorina. He only said that he has no money left, so we must call in the shop tomorrow to be paid.'

'Thanks for nothing,' Pietro growled. Glancing over his shoulder, he added, 'Remind me to double your rent.'

'*Sì,* signore.'

But the young man grinned as he said it. Evidently the idea of Pietro taking revenge was amusing.

'Rent?' Ruth queried.

'I own a few small places,' he conceded grudgingly.

Having glided a small distance down the Grand Canal, the little procession drifted into a turning, the gondola leading the way, the motor boat bringing up the rear, its occupants agog with interest.

The singer was strumming his mandolin, then bursting into song, not a romantic Italian song but a modern pop song currently in the charts.

'I warned him to be careful what he sang,' Pietro murmured.

But when the musician had finished there were cries for him to improve the performance. He looked uncertainly at Pietro, who glowered back.

'There's a limit to how much entertainment I'm prepared to provide for tourists,' he growled.

Ruth looked back at the motor boat.

'Where are you staying?' she asked, for the sake of friendly conversation.

'Don't know yet,' the jester replied. 'We just jumped on the train and came out here for a good time. Now we need a cheap hotel.'

'All the hotels are full,' Pietro called. 'You'd best go back.'

'But isn't there a travel agency that could help us?'

'No, there isn't.'

'Yes, there is,' Ruth urged. 'I know of one—'

'No, you don't,' Pietro said firmly.

'Yes, I do. It's in St Mark's Piazza—'

The rest of her words were lost as he grasped hold of her, hauled her close and silenced her mouth with his own.

It she hadn't been otherwise occupied Ruth could have laughed out loud. How to get him to kiss her again had been preoccupying her mind, and now she'd solved the problem very neatly. Just a little provocation had been enough to do it. She made a mental note to remember that.

Then all thought was blotted out in the pleasure of being in his arms, feeling his lips on hers, sensing the agonies of self-restraint that were torturing him as much as her. He wanted to kiss her but not like this, before an audience. He wanted to yield to the feelings that were driving him, evoking hers in return. Except that hers needed no prompting. She was as full of passion as he, yearning to respond to him fully, in a way that could only be done when they were alone.

She did her fervent best to let him know how she felt, but this wasn't the time or the place. The best could come later.

She sighed as he released her, caring for nothing except for the moment.

'I suppose that gave them something to talk about,' she said hazily.

'They're gone,' said the gondolier behind them.

It was true. The motor boat had turned away down another canal, leaving their gondola the only boat in sight. The singer was strumming away and beginning another song.

'He's singing Venetian, isn't he?' she asked. 'What do the words mean?'

Pietro began to translate,

'"We have all the beauty in the world. Secrets that no one else knows, Will be ours for ever. But do I mean Venice, Or our love?"'

'What a lovely song,' she murmured, her head leaning against him.

'Have you ever heard it before?'

'No,' she said, understanding his true meaning. 'Not from Gino or anyone.'

'I don't care about anyone else—just Gino.'

Ruth waited for him to kiss her again, but now he was looking at the water ahead, and she realised that he was suddenly uneasy. It was the men standing behind them, she realised. It would be different when they were really alone. For the moment it was enough to nestle against him in perfect contentment, and let things happen as they would.

Time no longer existed, if it had ever existed. Little canals came into view, leading away into darkness, then passing into other canals. From the distance came music and laughter, yet here they were almost alone.

'When did you last eat?' Pietro asked suddenly.

'I can't remember. I skipped breakfast and today was so busy, and then I went to the station and I forgot everything else.'

'Me too, and I'm hungry.'

'I'm *ravenous.*'

At his signal the gondolier rowed over to the bank and let them land on a small piazza, where lights dazzled from a few modest buildings. As he drifted off Pietro put his arm around her shoulders and led her to a tiny place, 'run by a friend of mine'.

As she'd expected and hoped the restaurant was neither expensive nor fashionable, being little more than a pizza parlour, with many dishes being cooked in plain sight. One chef was doing a stunt, tossing a 'pancake' higher and higher, to loud applause. When he'd finished he hailed the new-comers with a roar.

'Pietro—' The rest of his words were indistinguishable.

'*Ciao*, Sandro.'

Pietro turned out his pockets, indicating that he had no money, and the man made a gesture that clearly meant, 'So what?' The next moment they were being led to a table in the tiny garden at the back. Luckily the weather was warm for January, and they sat there in comfort while Sandro bustled out with a menu that contained fifty different pizzas.

'You pick what you want and Sandro makes each one up individually,' Pietro explained. 'He's a genius and these are his masterpieces.'

He was right. When the food arrived it was so delicious that neither spoke for several minutes. Then Pietro groaned.

'What's the matter? It's lovely,' Ruth protested.

'The food's fine. I was thinking of the day I've had.'

'Has the Baronessa been giving you a hard time?'

He gave her a speaking look.

'She spent most of the day lecturing me about the meaning of Carnival.'

'But doesn't she know you've lived here all your life?'

'If she does, she gives it less significance than

her "feelings". She's aiming to take part in the opening procession, although the arrangements were settled ages ago. She's relying on me to speak to the organisers. She says she's sure that I can do *anything* I set my mind to.'

'Compete with sighs and fluttering eyelashes?'

'Complete with everything. She keeps trying to get me alone so that she can exercise her "charms".' He closed his eyes.

'But surely a man of the world like you can cope with her easily?' she teased.

Pietro gave her a baleful look. 'It isn't funny.'

'It is,' she choked. 'It's terribly funny.'

He gave a reluctant grin. 'All right, it's funny. But being rude to women is an art I never quite mastered, and it's too late to start now. Besides, Franco is my friend.'

'I suppose you could just give her that deadly stare you once gave him.'

'It would just ricochet off her, and she'd give me one back. I'd back her against myself anyday.'

He began to laugh, the kind of full-hearted sound she'd never expected to hear from him. It was good to watch him covering his eyes with one hand and shaking with mirth.

'Anyway, it's your fault,' he said at last. 'You should have stayed there to protect me.'

The thought of this strong, attractive man

needing her protection made her chuckle again. She felt light-headed, finding amusement in everything, flying up to the stars.

'I'm sorry,' she said meekly. 'I didn't mean to desert you in the face of the enemy, but I never thought of it.'

'I'm surprised, given your low opinion of men.'

'What does that mean?'

'I remember hearing you talk about Salvatore Ramirez after that evening you spent with him and his wife. You said he was mostly window dressing—like most men.'

'Did I really say that?'

'You know you did. Your voice had a scathing note that made me curious.'

'I wasn't scathing,' she protested.

'You certainly didn't sound as though the male sex had greatly impressed you.'

'I can't think why.'

'Is that a real lapse of memory or a diplomatic one?'

'I think I must have been going more by my instincts than my experience,' she said, recalling his words of another time.

'So it's your instincts that tell you not to bother with men because we're all hopeless?'

'Mmm!' She considered. 'The idea occasionally strolls through my mind.'

'Shall I tell you what strolls through my mind?' he asked satirically. 'That when I found you in the rain that night I should have left you out there.'

'You wouldn't have done that. If I'd knocked on your door full of self-confidence and dressed in expensive clothes, you'd have sent me away with a flea in my ear, rain or no rain.'

He glared. 'I hope you're not suggesting that I'm a soft-hearted do-gooder who actually prefers creatures who need protecting.'

'Of course not,' she said, sounding shocked. 'I wouldn't dream of insulting you like that.'

'Because, to my mind, that's just another sort of arrogance.'

'Perhaps you are arrogant, in your own way,' she mused. 'Maybe I will insult you, just a little. Admit it. You took me in for the same reason you took Toni in.'

'Sure, you're just another lost dog. I look at you and Toni and I can hardly tell the difference.'

'That's easy. I'm hairier,' she said at once.

'Don't make me laugh while I'm eating,' he begged.

Not for the first time with Pietro, she discovered that the roads to a serious truth could lead through laughter. It was in his big, generous nature to reach out to the weak and vulnerable, and then be grumpy about it afterwards.

It was only recently that she had fully understood that she was made the same way. Where others saw his money and status, she saw his need, and longed to care for him as he cared for her. But this too had to be half concealed behind amusement. He was touchy.

'I love this,' she said suddenly. 'When the evening began, I had no idea it would end this way. That's the best kind of evening. Life should be unexpected.'

Right on cue the waiter appeared with the menu so that she could look through a series of dishes that she'd never seen before.

'They all look very unexpected,' she mused.

'The plain and simple ice cream is the best. My friends here make it themselves.'

'You choose for me.'

He selected a chocolate ice cream straight out of heaven, topped off with nuts, and ordered a bottle of champagne.

'Are we celebrating something?' she asked.

'I feel as if we ought to be,' he said enigmatically.

'You're right. We'll think of something later.'

They clinked glasses with an air of triumph.

'I feel as though Carnival has started already.' Ruth sighed happily. 'The time when people forget common sense and go wild. Ah, well!' She raised her champagne glass and intoned, 'There's always Lent to repent.'

'I can't imagine you ever repenting,' he mused. 'I think if you decided on something you'd go for it and accept the consequences.'

An echo skittered through her brain. Somewhere, quite recently, she'd heard that before. But then it was gone and she had no time to brood.

'I think I would,' she agreed. 'Whatever they were. If you don't reach out and seize life—you'd never know, would you? And that could be the most painful thing in the world, not knowing. That could be the worst thing that might ever happen to you, to go through life, wondering—'

So preoccupied was she with the thought that she was barely aware of him watching her from dark eyes, until he said, 'That won't happen, Ruth, I promise you. I'll get him back here, and make him help you.'

'Oh, yes, Gino!' For a moment she'd completely forgotten about him.

'Weren't you talking about him?'

'He's not the only thing in life,' she prevaricated. 'There are other things to wonder about, things it would be sad never to know.'

'Were you thinking of anything in particular?' he asked, watching her closely.

She thought for a moment. 'I'm not sure.' Then a brilliant smile illuminated her eyes. 'Is there any more champagne?'

CHAPTER TEN

AS THEY left the restaurant Pietro asked, 'Do you know where you are?'

'No,' Ruth said softly. 'I have no idea where I am. I'm completely lost.'

But being lost didn't seem so very terrible just now.

'Let's walk home,' she said. 'I don't care how far it is.'

'But it's no distance. A few corners and we're there.'

Even as he spoke she saw the top of the Rialto Bridge appear over the roofs.

'Oh,' she said, disappointed, for she had looked forward to the walk.

'We just have to cross the bridge and we're home.'

Shops lined the bridge on both sides and by day it was a hive of activity. Now the shops were shut, the lights were dimmed and couples huddled in the doorways. Some of them looked up to inspect the newcomers, and offered a murmured greeting, for they all knew him.

'You should be ashamed,' he told them. 'Carnival hasn't started yet.'

The voices floated back. 'Just getting a little practice— We want to be ready— The honour of Venice—'

Ruth reached up and slid an arm about his neck.

'Just doing my bit for the honour of Venice,' she murmured as she drew his mouth down to hers.

Now she was taking charge, telling him that they would do it her way because she'd been patient long enough. But how long was that? All her life, surely. It was strange how all the mystifying questions answered themselves when you were with the right man. Or perhaps it wasn't strange at all.

She was consumed with a sense of having come to the right place, standing here in the heart of Venice. She'd always been headed for this bridge, with this man. And wherever the road led afterwards, that too was her true destination.

Neither knew who made the first move, but in the next moment they were moving slowly over the bridge and into the little side street where he had first seen her.

They made almost no noise as they slipped into the building and up the stairs. Toni looked up as they came in, then settled back to sleep, so there was nobody to watch them as they went again into each other's arms, or to see his sudden moment of doubt.

'Ruth…Ruth…I don't know—'

'It doesn't matter,' she whispered. 'Don't try to think.'

As she spoke she drew her fingers gently down his face, looking up at him with eyes that loved everything she saw. She wondered if it could be the same for him, but for the moment it was enough that he held her, raining kisses on her lips, her eyes, her throat.

She had never experienced such feelings in her life before. Even with gaps in her memory she knew that. Instinct, stronger than reason, more powerful than memory, took over, telling her this man was unique, his effect on her was once in a lifetime, and she was going to open her heart to it, or live bereft for ever.

'Perhaps I ought to think,' he murmured. 'I'm looking after you. How can you be safe if I—?'

'Who says I want to be safe? Do *you* want that?'

He made an inarticulate sound that might have been a groan at his own helplessness. He tried to speak but, whatever he wanted to say, his hands had their own message, touching her feverishly, seeking her response despite the doubts that troubled him.

'Isn't this better than safety?' she murmured against his mouth.

'Yes!'

If she'd wanted to escape him then she couldn't have done. His arms suddenly became like chains, forbidding her to leave him, his hands were possessive, now holding her, now releasing her so that he could pull off her coat, tossing it away, then seeking her buttons, working on them, discovering the soft skin beneath.

Her bedroom door was just close enough for her to reach behind and turn the knob. A small step back and they were gliding through almost without realising.

Pietro guided her so that she was sitting, then lying on the bed, and he could rest his face against her exposed breasts. What was happening to him now shook him to the core. Not just desire, not just emotion, but the mystic combination of the two that was worth any sacrifice. If it had been in his power he would have made it last for ever, and counted the world well lost.

But the world wouldn't let itself be lost. It clung on to the edge of his consciousness, reminding him of the last time he'd come to the bed and felt her arms around him and her whisper of *'Te voja ben,'* in his ears.

He tensed as the unwelcome knowledge

invaded him. That had been on the first night, when she'd been half-unconscious, and she'd kissed him, thinking he was Gino. She had awoken directly afterwards and hadn't seemed to react. He'd sworn then never to let her know the truth, and until now he'd kept his vow.

But now—

'What is it?' Ruth asked, distressed as he gave a sudden heave. 'What's the matter?'

'How can you ask?' he choked, pulling away from her, 'Am I mad to be doing this?'

He got to his feet, almost staggering with the violence of his revulsion for himself.

'How can it be mad if it's what you want?' Ruth asked. 'What we both want?'

'Is that all that matters? What we want at this moment? What about later, the regrets?'

'Will you regret?' she asked quietly.

He had himself under control now, and said, 'I'll regret anything I do that hurts you.'

'I'm not worried about that—'

'But I have to be. You're not well, that's why you're here. You came to me for help and I—'

'Pietro, I'm not an invalid.'

'But neither are you completely well. It was only a few hours ago that you set off for the railway station to meet Gino, thinking of nothing but him. If he'd been there—what would you have felt?'

'I don't know.'

'Exactly. Maybe you love him, maybe not, but you don't know. And until you've had a chance to find out the answer to that, I have no right to—' He shuddered. 'What was I thinking of?'

'Perhaps you wanted me,' she said with a quick spurt of anger, doing up her buttons quickly. She knew now that he wouldn't return to her.

'Of course I want you. If there was nothing else standing between us I could go back to my bad old ways and take—'

'Don't you dare say it,' she interrupted him. 'Don't you dare say "take advantage of me" like I was a wimp who couldn't speak for herself.'

'That's not what I meant.'

'I think it is,' she said fiercely.

'I meant only that you're vulnerable. We both know why. For me to take—take what you have to give,' he amended hastily, seeing murder in her eyes, 'would be unforgivable.' He added in a low voice, 'And I've done enough unforgivable things in my life.'

She wanted to say, 'Would it be unforgivable to love me?' but she wouldn't let herself do that. Love was the word she didn't dare to use, although the conviction of it was growing in her own heart. He wasn't ready to love her. He might never be ready. But she could wait.

'I don't believe you've ever done anything unforgivable,' she said.

'What the hell do you know about it?'

Ruth jumped at the sound of his voice, not merely the sudden volume but at the note of ferocity. It cut through her like a razor and gave her a terrifying sensation, as though he'd turned on her the same look he'd turned on Franco.

'What do you know?' he repeated in a voice that was less harsh but still biting. 'Do you know about my life, what my experience has been? Do you know *me?*'

'I thought I did,' she said softly.

'You know no more of me than I do of you. We play this little game in which you're three people, but it's not a game. There's a tragic reality beneath it, and what would you think of me if I betrayed your trust? Do you know how vulnerable you are here, with me?'

'I never feel that way. I trust you—'

'Why? What reason have I ever given you to trust me?'

'All this time you've cared for me, and never harmed me—'

He gave a crack of mirthless laughter.

'I was biding my time, waiting to pounce at the right moment. Can you be sure that's not the truth?'

Dumbly she shook her head. The pain that was rising in her was too great for words.

'No, you can't because you know nothing of me.' He leaned towards her and his eyes were cold. 'I could treat you any way I liked and you'd have no comeback. In this city who'd listen to you against me?'

Something in his bleak hostility caused her own temper to rise.

'Of course, I should have realised,' she snapped. 'They'd think you were reverting to type. Casanova reborn, that's what they used to say about you, isn't it?'

'You've heard the stories? Good! Maybe you'll see sense.'

'Yes. I've heard the stories of your flaming youth. And how! You probably made half of them up.'

'I promise I didn't need to. I behaved every bit as badly as they say, and a few more things nobody ever got to hear of, luckily.'

'So, of course nobody would listen to me. They'd say I was lucky you even looked at me. Only you're not Casanova anymore.'

'You don't know what I am,' he said roughly. 'If you know that much, you ought to have more sense than to be here with me now.'

'I'm not a fool. You can say what you like. I think you can be trusted.'

'And how would you know? Has your experience been so extensive? Did Gino teach you about trust? I don't think so. What about before him?'

It was cruel, it was appallingly brutal, and she reeled with shock, closing her eyes against the agony that he'd inflicted deliberately. She had no doubt of that. He saw the movement and reached out a hand to her, only to snatch it back before she could see it. When she opened her eyes it was to find him staring at her from eyes that gave nothing away.

'Nothing like this will ever happen again,' he said in a dead voice. 'You have my word on that. Goodnight.'

Pietro walked out, closing the door firmly behind him. A moment later Ruth heard his own door being locked.

She clenched and unclenched her hands, filled with bitter rage at that final insult. He'd locked her out like some floozy who didn't come up to standard. She wanted to scream and throw something against the wall.

There was no point in even lying down, so she sat in the darkness, looking out of the window at the Grand Canal, numb with despair.

She didn't recognise the man who'd attacked her so coldly tonight, but she could guess what he was thinking and feeling; scorn for her lack of control in throwing herself at him, contempt at her arrogance in thinking she had the power to charm him.

She'd once made a joke about Serafina treating her like Cinderella, but how could Cinderella be so foolish as to think she could really charm the Prince, except for five minutes? That was a fairy tale.

She must leave, of course. As soon as she could will herself to move she would begin to pack. Anything would be better than facing him again.

But then a water bus passed under the Rialto Bridge, its lights gleaming across the canal, briefly illuminating the windows of Pietro's room where they jutted out slightly from the rest of the building. It was only a moment, but it was enough for Ruth to see the man standing there, his face a frozen mask of misery that mirrored her own.

She stepped back at once, but she knew he hadn't seen her. He had no eyes for the outside world, only for some earthquake that was taking place inside him.

Ruth groaned as she realised her blunder. Wrapped in her own feelings, she had been blind to the effect on him. In her relief at breaking free of Gino she'd forgotten that Pietro was far from free of Lisetta.

Now she saw the whole conversation differently. Pietro had tried to be kind, speaking of his duty to care for her, but the truth was that he didn't want her. Not really. Not beyond one night's basic pleasure. He still yearned for his dead wife, and no other woman would be allowed to come between them. So he'd crushed his desire, treating it as something unworthy of notice, until tonight, when she'd forced everything out into the open.

Not forced it out, she thought, cringing at her own stupidity. *More like kicked it out with hobnailed boots.*

Tonight he'd had to abandon kindness and turn on her to make her get the point. And she had only herself to blame.

I've got to get out, she thought frantically. *I mustn't be here tomorrow. I can't look him in the eye.*

Packing was a problem. The small suitcase she'd had when she arrived was useless for all her new clothes.

'Plastic bags,' she muttered. 'In the kitchen.'

She was out there in a moment scrabbling around in the drawers.

'What are you doing?'

Pietro was standing in the doorway, frowning.

'I'm leaving,' she said. 'I just need to finish packing, and I'll be gone. You don't have to see me again. Now if you'll just stand aside—'

He didn't move.

'Put them back and go to bed,' he said firmly. 'You're not leaving this house.'

'Hey, who are you giving orders?'

His mouth quirked slightly at the corner.

'It comes from being a count, from the oldest family in Venice,' he said lightly, 'surrounded by wealth and privilege. You tend to get used to people doing as they're told. Reprehensible, but there it is.'

'And if don't do as I'm told?' she challenged.

'Well, I did tell you once I had this fantasy about tossing you into the Grand Canal.'

He was a semblance of his old self again, armoured in ironic defensiveness, even smiling. It was a relief, and yet she knew a strange sense of loss. Once more she was shut out.

'I can't stay,' she repeated.

'Why? Because I behaved badly? I give you my word it'll never happen again.'

He was so clever, she thought bitterly, taking it all on himself, while they both knew the truth: that she had fallen in love with him, a man who could never love her.

'You once accused me of being too ready to protect everyone,' he said.

'I didn't exactly—'

'Well, you're right. That's how I am, and sometimes I get a bit carried away. I convince myself that nothing can be done right unless it's done my way, not an amiable characteristic. In fact it can verge on bullying if it's not controlled, but it's how I'm made. And when I've taken a job on I see it through to the end. Tonight—'

He stopped and she held her breath.

'I decided to care for you until you were well, but tonight I nearly forgot that promise and drove you away by my clumsiness. Blame Venice. It has that effect on people. Even me. It's like setting out in a gondola and finding yourself in another universe.'

'Yes,' she said, for that was how it had been.

They had been carried to an alternative existence where they laughed with each other, opened their hearts, rejoiced together. And she should have seen that, in the end, the gondola would reach the unfriendly shore.

'You won't be ready to go until you've seen Gino,' Pietro was saying. 'And I'd commit a crime if I let you go out into a hostile world before you're ready to cope. Don't do that to me, Ruth. I have quite enough on my conscience as it is. If you stay, I promise not to embarrass you again. You'll be quite safe.'

And there it was, the whole disaster neatly repackaged into a shape they could live with, life and emotion stripped from it. All love quenched. Polite. Dead.

'Come,' he said, taking the plastic bags from her and putting them back in the drawer. 'Let's say it didn't happen.'

'It didn't happen,' she echoed in a voice as empty as his own.

'Good. Now, we've got a busy few days in front of us, so get some sleep.'

That would be impossible, she thought. But she did manage to drop off eventually and awoke late. Pietro had already left when she went out, and Minna told her that he'd called home to ask her to take some papers to the shop.

She took the papers but found that he wasn't at work either, although he'd left a pile of messages with Mario about things he wanted her to do. She appreciated the subtlety with which he left her alone while keeping her busy.

Halfway through the morning the boatmen came in for the money Pietro had promised them the night before. Mario was ready with the full envelopes Pietro had left in his care, and the young men opened them with whistles of appreciation that changed to significant looks as they recognised Ruth. Now she was glad Pietro wasn't there.

She went home alone and ate supper without expecting him.

'He's always so busy at this time of the year,'

Minna observed. 'He says Carnival is big business, except, of course, last year when he got out of the city for the sake of his wife.'

'Didn't she like Carnival?' Ruth asked.

'Oh, yes, but she was coming close to her time and he wanted her to be away from all the noise and bustle. They went out to the estate to let her rest, and this place was almost empty, so many of the servants were given time off to visit their families. They returned in March, and that was when she gave birth and died.'

Minna gave a big sigh. Then she added, 'Did he say what time he'd be home tonight?'

'I haven't spoken to him, but Mario thought he would be late.'

She finished the evening in her room, working at her translation, trying to be oblivious to all else. If Pietro came home now he mustn't find her waiting up for him, which would be awkward for both of them. Besides, she assured herself that she was too involved in her work to listen for his key in the door.

But that sound had not come when she put away her books, went to bed and turned out the lamp.

In the *calle* below a man patiently watched the light in the window. When it went out he stood a while longer before walking away and vanishing into the dark streets.

* * *

It was two days before Ruth saw Pietro again, and it was less traumatic than she'd feared because it happened in the middle of one of Serafina's tantrums. Having transformed the palazzo as much as she could, the Baronessa set her heart on moving into it at the very start of Carnival, instead of waiting for the ball, near the end of the festivities. Shrewdly choosing a moment when Pietro was away, she arrived unannounced with a mountain of luggage, which she ordered to be taken upstairs.

Ruth immediately got on the phone to Pietro in the shop and explained what had happened.

'I'm on my way,' he said. 'Try to stop them murdering each other until I get there.'

Serafina was livid to find the count and countess's private suite locked, refusing to accept Minna's explanation that this was according to Pietro's orders. Another set of rooms was being prepared, and would be available in a few days. Serafina proceeded to have a hissy fit that passed in legend, Minna stoutly refused to be intimidated and Ruth tried vainly to keep the non-existent peace. It ended with Serafina being spitefully rude to her at the precise moment that Pietro appeared.

What followed was entertaining. Serafina used all her wiles on Pietro, to no effect. Politely but implacably he repeated that she would be welcome in a few days but not today, and the suite of rooms she wanted was off limits.

Franco arrived and joined in the fray. Pietro repeated himself again until Franco understood that he meant it. Although stupid, he wasn't quite as stupid as his wife, and he finally swept her off, in high dudgeon, to Venice's most expensive hotel where Pietro had taken the precaution of booking them a suite in advance.

The servants, who had gathered to watch, roared and applauded Pietro, who gave them an ironic bow. The spat seemed to have cheered him. Having checked that Minna wasn't upset, he turned his attention to Ruth.

'I'm fine,' she assured him cheerfully. 'I haven't enjoyed myself so much for ages. Did you see her face?'

That set everyone off laughing again, and Ruth found that the atmosphere between herself and Pietro had calmed down to normal. There were too many other things to worry about now. The other night might never have happened.

A few days later Serafina and Franco took over the rooms allocated to them, where their costumes had been installed in readiness. Serafina had been largely thwarted in her bid to turn the palazzo into a Hollywood mansion, but she'd hung enough glittering decoration to make Pietro shudder.

They were to be dressed in the eighteenth-century style, as was normal for Carnival. Franco would wear knee breeches and a flare coat, neither of which did any favours to his overfed body. Serafina's dress was of scarlet satin, lavishly embroidered with glittering gold thread, and cut low in the bosom. She insisted on parading before the household, accompanied by Franco, bursting with pride.

'Don't worry,' Pietro told Ruth when they had escaped. 'You'll take the shine out of her.'

'Me? I'm not going to be there.'

'You don't think I'm going to endure it alone, do you? You'll be there, and you'll wear the costume I'm having sent over for you.' He caught her looking at him and added hastily, 'I mean, please will you wear the costume?'

'It's all right. I guess being *il conte* is a hard habit to break.'

'I'm doing my best.'

'What's my costume like?'

'Ivory brocade.'

'You mean I don't get scarlet satin?' she asked wickedly. 'Shame!'

'You'll drive me too far.'

All was well, she told herself. They were cracking jokes again, and that was surely the best possible thing.

Even a subdued Serafina was someone to avoid, and after she moved in Ruth began spending more time in the palazzo library, which, she rightly guessed, was the last place the Baronessa would want to visit. It was a useful chance to practise her improving Italian, especially as she found one book both in the original language and an English translation.

It was a historical record of the great families of Venice, including the Bagnellis and also the Alluccis. After an initial hesitation Ruth delved into the story of generations of the Allucci family. It stopped before the birth of Lisetta Allucci who had married Pietro Bagnelli, but Ruth found something else that intrigued her, and sat considering it for a long time.

She was still thoughtful when she went to bed which was, perhaps, why her dreams took a strange turn that night.

There was Lisetta, arrayed in her bridal finery. But that picture vanished, to be replaced by the earlier one, taken when she was thirteen, playing dice, staking everything on one throw.

Ruth opened her eyes and sat up.

That's just what I did the other night, she thought. *Everything staked on one all-or-nothing throw. That was the chance I took, and the answer was nothing. So, shut up complaining Ruth Three.*

You're beginning to sound like Ruth Two, and you know what I think of her.

After a moment she even managed to say ironically, 'I guess I'm just not a very good gambler, but how was I to know that? I'm still getting used to myself.'

She wished she could have shared that joke with Pietro, but there were things they couldn't say now.

Carnival had arrived, the time of masks and masques, of jollity, eating, drinking and merry sin. The merrier and more sinful, the better.

It began at precisely midday with the *Volo dell'Angelo*, in which a woman dressed as an angel scattered flowers over the crowd in St Mark's Piazza.

Minna had secured a small revenge against Serafina by suggesting that her talents were underused in the Carnival, and she should have insisted that this role had gone to her. Serafina had promptly demanded that Franco secure it for her, which Franco was determined to do, until Pietro hastily explained that the angel reached the piazza by gliding down a rope hung from the top of St Mark's bell tower, over three hundred feet up.

After that Serafina's enthusiasm waned, and she looked at Minna with glowering eyes. Minna didn't look at her at all.

Day after day St Mark's piazza was filled with musicians, acrobats, clowns and people who just enjoyed wearing fancy dress. They performed or watched others perform, laughed, sang, kissed, then went wandering off along the *calles*, their cheerful sounds floating back behind them.

Officially this was the celebration of winter giving way to spring, but it was February and, to the last minute, Ruth feared a cold snap, but Mario assured her that nature always obliged, and so it proved. There was even the odd burst of sun.

For such a great tourist attraction Pietro was kept busy. In addition to his other interests he had shares in a couple of hotels, both of which were packed with visitors, and hosting galas of their own. Being kind-hearted, he briefed Mario to join in these events and report back to him. Naturally this entailed dressing up and Mario selected the 'devil' costume Ruth had seen him wear the mask of on the first day, and which had mysteriously failed to appeal to anyone else.

'Probably because the two of you have been keeping it out of sight,' Pietro murmured. 'Go on, Mario, and be sure to take notes.'

'Eh?'

'About the party,' Ruth reminded him gently.

'Oh—yes. The party.'

They managed to keep straight faces as he

swaggered off, looking sophisticated and devil-may-care. His note-taking was sketchy to say the least, but from the odd remark they later judged that he'd enjoyed himself in ways that left no time for note-taking.

Pietro took part in very few events. Ruth knew that he attended a concert of classical Venetian music one evening and made brief appearances at other, fairly sedate events. But apart from that he meant to keep aloof, except for the gala ball in his own home.

Ruth's costume, when it arrived, was a dream of elegance and luxury, made of lavishly embroidered ivory satin. Now she was glad of her height, which made it easier to carry off the wide hoops that supported the skirt. The front was heavily decorated with lace and ribbons, cunningly interspersed with little jewels that had been sewn in and which glistened tantalisingly.

They might almost have been diamonds, Ruth thought, inspecting them closely. But that was impossible. They must simply be very well-cut glass.

At first she was relieved that the bosom wasn't cut as low as Serafina's, being conscious that she had less to show off. But when she tried on the gown she had to admit that this part of her was unimpressive.

Minna came to her rescue on the night of the ball, showing her a trick learned in her youth by which her breasts could be manoeuvred together and upwards, resulting in a display that was impressive while still managing to be decent, even if only just.

There was also a white wig that fitted her head snugly, with one curl drooping elegantly down onto her shoulder. Ruth was undecided whether to wear this, but finally decided that she would. It gave her a new look, and she wondered if there would be a Ruth Four before the night was out.

Then came the mask of ivory satin, covering most of her face except her mouth.

'The pleasure of a mask is the sins it can hide,' Gino had told her. 'At one time the Venetian Republic passed a decree forbidding masks except at Carnival and during official banquets. The penalty for disobeying could be two years in gaol.'

'Two years?' she'd echoed, aghast.

He'd laughed, standing before her in knee breeches and flared coat of black brocade, with the Bagnelli crest on the sleeves. Surely, she'd thought, he must be the most handsome young man on earth.

'The city fathers were very determined to stamp out immorality,' Gino had informed her solemnly. 'It didn't work, of course. Most of the fun of life comes from immorality—' he slipped on a black satin mask, leaning down to touch his mouth against hers, whispering '—and if there's one thing Venetians know about, it's enjoying life.'

That had been this time last year, when they had spent a few days of Carnival together before she had had to leave. He'd seen her off at the station, the same station where he'd left her standing recently, and they had parted with vows of eternal love.

Where was he now? Did it matter?

There was a knock at the door, and Minna's voice called, 'Pietro says are you ready?'

'I'm just coming.'

Slowly she got to her feet, checking her appearance in the mirror.

'You look wonderful,' Minna said. Dropping her voice, she added, 'He will lose his heart to you.'

'No, Minna, it's not like that,' Ruth said hastily. 'I'm just helping him out as part of my job.'

'Of course you are.'

She helped Ruth ease the magnificent skirt out of the door. From down below came the sound of the orchestra tuning up as Ruth made her way slowly down the corridor.

Then she froze.

Gino was walking towards her.

CHAPTER ELEVEN

SUDDENLY Ruth's heart was thundering, although with what feeling she couldn't be sure. It should have been delight, but it felt more like dread.

Gino had returned. He was here, advancing on her.

He looked just as he had last year, the black brocade costume, the mask that concealed most of his face, and she froze as he grew nearer. Then he spoke.

'Ruth, what's the matter?'

It was Pietro's voice. She let out a long gasp and steadied herself against the wall.

'You!' she exclaimed.

'Of course it's me.' He looked closely at her face. 'Who did you think it was?'

'Gino. I saw him in that costume last year. For a moment I thought—'

'So that's it. I guess he borrowed it because of this.' Pietro indicated the Bagnelli crest on the sleeves. 'Part of his impersonation. I'm sorry, I didn't mean to startle you.'

'No, I'm just being silly. It's only that I was thinking of him just before—something he told me, about masks, and people not being allowed to wear them except at Carnival.'

'Because you can get away with so much behind a mask,' Pietro supplied. 'That about sums up the Venetian attitude—get away with what you can, and worry about the consequences when you're caught, which you probably won't be as long as you keep your mask on.'

His light tone had its effect, and she relaxed.

'So while I'm masked I can have the time of my life,' she riposted.

'That's the spirit.'

She twirled around so that her magnificent skirts flared out.

'Will I do?'

'You'll be the belle of the ball.'

'Don't let Serafina hear you say that.'

He laughed, but inwardly he was cursing Gino. He wished he hadn't witnessed her face when she first caught sight of himself down the corridor, but he had, plus a lot of things that had dismayed him. He'd seen her shock, the way she'd stood still, holding on to the wall, shattered by the sight of the man who still dominated her thoughts and feelings.

She'd recovered, laughing, putting a brave face on it as she always did. But from now on everytime she looked at him she would see Gino as well, or perhaps only Gino.

Tonight was going to be a test of endurance.

But there was no time to brood over this. Down below the guests were beginning to arrive, ushered in by Franco's stewards who carried away their gorgeous cloaks. From the far end of the corridor Serafina appeared on Franco's arm, simpering at the sight of Pietro, then leaving Franco behind to hurry forward and give a deep curtsey that displayed her advantages to the full.

'Are you going to take me in to the ball?' she wittered.

Franco, realising that he was going to be deserted, bowed low to Ruth and offered her his arm.

'Dear lady, I don't know who you are, but I know you are beautiful,' he declaimed.

Realising that he hadn't recognised her, Ruth curtseyed and took his arm. Pietro, forestalled in his attempt to escape Serafina, yielded to the inevitable and offered her his own arm.

In this way the four of them proceeded down the grand staircase into the glittering ballroom, now filled with guests in various styles of costume. There were a few clowns, but most of them had spent a fortune on eighteenth-century garb, glittering with jewels. The men were in knee breeches, the women in crinolines, and many wore powdered wigs.

Ruth was glad that Pietro had decided not to wear a wig, hiding his dark hair. It would have spoilt him somehow, whereas now, among all these pretty creatures, his masculinity was emphasised.

There were some flashes of light as they left the last step, and Ruth realised that Serafina had invited photographers. No wonder she wanted to be seen in Pietro's company.

The music swelled, Pietro bowed and led her into the waltz. Franco and Ruth followed, then all the others.

She discovered that she'd been right about enjoying a new identity. After Franco came more men, flirting, admiring, and she danced with them all, in the spirit of Carnival.

Some of the dancing was eighteenth-century style, which alarmed her until she realised how simple it was. The man and woman stood side by side, arms outstretched, hand in hand, advancing, retreating, circling each other in stately fashion. When her partners realised that she was new to this they guided her, and she soon relaxed. After that she danced every dance.

'When will it be my turn?' Pietro demanded when their paths happened to cross.

'When *il conte* has done his duty,' she riposted.

'You're supposed to be chaperoning me, saving me from Serafina and her sisters under the skin.'

'Don't be such a spoilsport. Surely Cinderella is allowed to enjoy the ball too?'

'As long as it's understood that when you leave, I leave.'

'But I'm enjoying myself far too much to leave.'

She glided away, taking a hand that was held out to her, with only the vaguest idea whose it was.

'Be careful—' Pietro started to say, but found himself talking to empty air.

Supper was lavishly served on long tables with fine china and crystal glasses. At the head of the table Pietro played the perfect host, seeming to give the guests all his attention while managing to search for Ruth at the same time. She didn't eat at the table but drifted around among other guests who were wandering through the palazzo, and Pietro's glimpses of her were infrequent.

But then he caught a glimpse of something that drove everything else out of his head.

He could have sworn he saw Toni's face peering through a doorway. Someone immediately passed in front and when they had gone there was no sign of Toni, but a moment later he saw the dog again.

Evidently he'd slipped out while Minna wasn't looking. Pietro decided he should be rounded up and sent back without delay, and he rose from the table, excusing himself to his guests.

But when he went out into the corridor there was no sign of Toni. Nor was anyone else around.

Then, from somewhere he heard the whispered words, 'Come with me, my darling. I'm waiting for you.'

Entranced, he followed the voice, so full of beauty and mystery that he felt it could lead him anywhere. It came again.

'This way, my darling.'

The corridor led to another, narrower, less grand, one where few people went. He followed, seeking he knew not what.

'Come with me—come with me—'

In the heart of the building lay a small garden, surrounded on all sides, and reached by a long staircase that went around three inner sides. The cool air on his face told him he was nearing this sanctuary, and then he was out on the staircase, and the mystery was explained.

At the foot of the stair, as he'd half expected, was a figure in ivory brocade, her face masked, her air as enticing as her words. But it was not himself, or any man, that she was trying to entice. She was calling Toni, who was slowly descending the stairs to the garden, following the sweet call of that voice, as was his master.

'Poor Toni,' she cooed. 'Did everyone forget about your walk? And you're desperate to spend a penny, aren't you? Come along, there's a nice little flower bed down here that'll do you nicely. And don't worry, I won't tell anyone.'

Pietro stood back in the shadows, watching as Toni went down to her and took her advice, nestling against her afterwards as she produced a biscuit.

Pietro regarded her with fascinated disbelief. Behind them was a ballroom full of men eager to dance and flirt with her, and they might not have existed for all the notice she took. The disgraceful mutt had all her attention, and clearly considered that it was his right.

'Come on,' she said at last. 'I'll take you back to bed—oh, Minna, there you are.'

The housekeeper had bustled out from under the arches that surrounded the garden, and took charge of the dog.

'I'm sorry. I don't know how he got out,' she fussed.

'It doesn't matter. He'll be all right now.'

Minna vanished with Toni, and Pietro waited for the ivory clad figure to mount the stairs. Instead she leaned back against the wall, gazing up to the stars. Pietro thought a little smile hovered on her lips, but he couldn't be sure.

And if it were there, for whom was it meant?

Behind that mask were her eyes open or closed, and, if closed, who filled her dreams?

Adjusting his mask over his face, he went quietly down a few steps until he was standing just above her. She heard him and turned her head, but now he could just discern that her eyes were still closed.

'It's only me,' he said, leaving 'me' unspecified. 'I wondered why a woman leaves the ballroom where she's enjoying such a triumph.'

She gave a soft, knowing laugh that made him clutch a stone ledge beside him.

'And why should the host leave a ball where the triumph is his?' she teased.

'He came in search of her.'

'But perhaps she wanted to be alone,' Ruth objected.

'Then she must resign herself to not having her wish. A beautiful woman will never be allowed solitude.'

'But maybe she isn't beautiful beneath the mask. How can he tell?'

'He doesn't need to see her face, because he knows that her heart is gentle and loving, and no vulnerable creature has ever turned to her in vain.'

'That's charming, but what does it have to do with beauty?'

'It is the only beauty that counts,' he said softly.

She was disconcerted, but recovered herself to say, 'Why, what a thing to say at Carnival!'

'True. We should think only of the most fleeting kind of beauty, shouldn't we? But hers will never fade. Even when she looks—' a smile of remembrance touched his mouth '—like a drowned rat, her true loveliness is always there for the man who can appreciate it—if she chooses to show it to him.'

'You mean—perhaps she doesn't?'

'There might be barriers between them that he can't tear down alone, only with her help.'

'And you think she would refuse to give it?' Ruth asked with soft urgency.

'Who knows? Her mind and heart are hidden from him, perhaps even from herself.'

'That's true,' she murmured.

'When she understands the truth—who knows what that truth will be? Or if there will be only one truth?'

She could have continued this all night. To be standing here in the moonlight, fencing with him, seeming to talk lightly yet touching the subjects that haunted them, then dancing away before danger threatened, this filled her with a kind of ecstasy. She felt he was letting her look into his heart while gently questioning her own.

From above them came the sound of music

from the ballroom, faintly, then louder as the orchestra struck up a new tune. The sudden awareness broke the spell and made them move slightly away from each other.

'You should return to your guests,' she said.

'We'll return together.'

He held out his hand and she placed hers in it so that he could lead her up the stairs into the corridor. The music, closer now, seemed to enclose them.

He stopped to listen, then put out his hand, sliding it determinedly about her waist, drawing her close into a waltz.

'A man must take his chances while he can,' he murmured provocatively.

She laughed, and felt him tense as her breath brushed his face. They were close now, as they had been on the night they had so nearly made love, before he had rejected her. But this time they were not themselves, although neither could have said with certainty who they were.

Who knows what the truth will be? he had said.

Moving dream-like in his arms, Ruth felt that only one truth could ever matter again.

But there was danger in that. The world would intrude. Even now she heard it from the far end of the corridor. Doors were flung open, revellers poured out, laughing and singing, shattering the dream. She must escape.

Pietro, forced back to being a good host, hailed the other guests as politely as he could manage, and saw them go scurrying away, seeking dark corners where they could be alone. With a sigh of relief he turned back to Ruth.

But she had gone. He was alone in the dark corridor, wondering if it had all been a dream.

When he returned to the ball she was dancing with another man.

The festivities went on into the small hours, and to him every moment was interminable. Serafina dragged out the goodbyes for ever, but finally the last guest was gone, and even she fell silent, eyeing Franco balefully. For once his attention wasn't on her, but on 'the mystery woman' who'd vanished but lingered in his thoughts.

'I just wish I knew who she was,' he sighed.

'It was Ruth,' Pietro informed him coldly. 'The wig and the mask concealed her identity very well.'

'Ruth?' Serafina echoed in disgust. 'But she's only a—'

With Pietro's eyes on her she was suddenly afraid.

'Pure Carnival,' Franco said ecstatically.

A mystery woman, Pietro mused. That was exactly what she was, and it was driving him mad.

Smiling determinedly, he escorted Franco and Serafina upstairs to their rooms, pretended not to hear their hints about staying a few more days, bid them goodnight and returned thankfully to his own little corner.

To his relief he found Ruth there, having discarded the glorious dress and donned shirt and trousers to eat a prosaic dish of pasta. She bore no resemblance to the vision in satin brocade who had tormented him, and for a moment he even wondered. But only for a moment.

'Where did you vanish to?' he demanded.

'Oh, here and there. You saw me around.' She sighed happily. 'I wouldn't have thought there were so many attractive men in the world. At least, I think they were attractive. Once the mask came off—who knows?'

Her shrug was eloquent.

'I believe a few masks were removed at the end of the evening,' he said.

'It might be better if they hadn't been. Better to enjoy the dream than face the reality.'

He turned on her swiftly. 'Do you really mean that?'

'Oh, I don't know. How should I know what I mean after an evening like that? It's Carnival, and, like a good Venetian, I'm making the most of it, because it'll be my last.'

She cleared away her dish, taking it into the kitchen. When she returned Pietro had removed the elegant black coat and the long waistcoat that went beneath it.

'You don't know it'll be your last,' he said.

'Yes, I do. I've been making plans, and it's time I was leaving.'

There was a businesslike note in her voice that was unfamiliar to him.

'What about Gino?' he asked curiously.

'He's not coming back. It's time I banished him from my life and managed without him. There's got to be a new life somewhere, away from him—away from you.'

She said the last words softly and he gave her a sharp look.

'You're going *now*?' He filled the last word with meaning. 'After tonight?'

'Tonight didn't really happen.'

'Are you still blaming me for the other evening?' he demanded.

'When you wouldn't make love to me? It's not blame. It's just that I've finally started to see things straight. The dream was lovely, but the reality has to be faced. I'm sorry I gave you so much trouble about that, Pietro.'

'I don't quite understand you.'

'Don't you? It's plain enough. I did something stupid. I fell in love with you. There, I've admitted it. I'm free of Gino. He only matters for the things he can tell me. The one I love is you. Couldn't you tell—tonight?'

'Then that really was you?' he said with a touch of relief. 'For a moment—'

'Yes, it was me—one of me. All the others are being very sensible because they have to be, now. Don't be embarrassed. I know I must leave. I won't intrude on your marriage.'

'Since my wife is dead, what marriage?'

'The marriage that still fills your life because she's the only one you can love. It's all right, I've finally faced that. All you want is to shut yourself up in this mausoleum with Lisetta, because that way you can pretend she isn't dead.'

'You know nothing about it.'

'I know you're dying inside, and you're letting it happen. You're *glad* for it to happen because you think you can be with her again. But you can't, Pietro, you can't. She's dead and you can't bring her back.'

His eyes seemed to burn in their sockets. 'I don't need to bring her back,' he raged. 'She isn't dead. She's here, everywhere, all the time. Every door I open, I know she's on the other side. She's in every room I enter. When I dream, she's there. When I awake, she's there. In my last moment, as I fall asleep, she whispers that she's there.'

'And you can't wait to find her,' she challenged.

'I don't have to find her, she finds me. She always will.'

'Was she there tonight?' she flashed, and had her answer in the tension in his face.

'Yes,' he said hoarsely.

'But must you always give in to it?' she cried. 'Is there nothing for us?'

His face softened. 'There could have been everything for us—if things had been different. Do you want me to say that I love you? Is that what you're waiting for, to hear the words?'

'Can you say them?' she asked, hardly breathing.

'I—' For a long moment he stood there, his face distraught, his whole being on the edge of words that tortured him, while she watched, knowing that her life depended on the next few moments. Then—

'No!' The word burst from him almost as an explosion. 'No, I don't love you.'

But suddenly her heart leapt and she looked at him with shining eyes. He loved her. By the very vehemence of his denial she knew the truth.

'I think you do,' she said simply. 'Is it so hard to say it?'

'It's impossible. It can't be true. It mustn't be true.'

'But she's dead. You're free now.'

'Free?' The word was like a knife. 'I'll never be

free, and do you know why? Because she's dead. Because I killed her. There's no escape from that prison, and nor should there be. Why should I escape? *I killed her.*'

The words shocked her to silence. Whatever she'd expected, it wasn't this.

'But that can't be true,' she choked at last. 'She died in childbirth.'

'She died bearing a child, a child she should never have been asked to bear. She wasn't strong enough, but she pretended that she was, and I pretended to believe her. I wanted that child. The terrible truth is that I wanted it more than I wanted her, and she knew it.

'She never considered herself for a moment. Everything was for me. There was nothing she wouldn't have done to please me, because she knew—' He paused and shuddered so violently that Ruth could feel it. 'She knew that I didn't love her.'

His voice was full of bleak despair as he said the final words, and then a deadly silence fell, as though the end of the world had come, and there was nothing left.

'Surely you must have loved her a little,' she said. 'You married her.'

'I had a kind of fondness for her. She was sweet and gentle and I'd known her most of my life. I showed you the pictures of us as children.'

'The dice game,' she said. 'Yes, I remember.'

'When she grew up I danced with her, always feeling like her brother because I'd known her for so long. It never occurred to me that she—'

He broke off awkwardly.

Ruth didn't need to hear him say all the words to be able to follow the progress. It had started with childish hero-worship, turned into a teenage crush, and then into womanly love. And he, with fairly typical male blindness, had been aware of it only distantly without seeing the implications or the danger.

'When I started to notice girls in a big way, I went a little mad,' Pietro resumed. 'I was the son of Count Bagnelli. I could indulge myself with any girl I liked. Don't ever let anyone tell you that aristocracy doesn't matter in the modern world. It counts as much as it ever did.'

Ruth thought of Franco and Serafina, and knew he was right.

'A title, or just the prospect of one, gives you a freedom no other man has,' Pietro continued. 'I won't go into details about how badly I behaved. Let's just say that I took what was offered, accepting it as my right. I'm not proud of that.'

She remembered Jessica saying, 'He only slept with the best, very stylish ladies. But they had to be outstanding, not just beautiful, but with a certain "something extra", to make him proud.'

And even Mario had wistfully implied that Pietro could take his pick.

But while Pietro connected his sexual success with his title she knew that his personal attractions must have played a big part. The title was a bonus, but it was the man himself who would make a woman's heart beat faster.

'So you had a colourful life,' she said gently. 'So do millions of young men with no money or title. You must have slowed down in the end.'

'My father had a heart attack. I was away at the time and it was Lisetta who called me. Against all the odds he survived and returned home, and she volunteered to come and look after him. He was fond of her and she seemed able to make him relax. I was grateful to her.

'But although he made a sort of recovery, we knew he didn't have very long. He said that before he died he wanted to see me "decently married", as he put it. He wanted to be at my wedding, and to know that at least there was a child on the way. He thought it was time I "chose a suitable bride", as though we were still in the nineteenth century.

'It didn't seem so strange to me. His own marriage to my mother had been arranged this way. They were civil, but not madly in love, and to me that was normal.

'He was dying, and I couldn't bear to deny him

his last wish, so I agreed. It was he who suggested Lisetta. We knew each other well, I liked her, and thought she liked me. At that time I had no idea that her feelings went deeper.'

'Didn't it come out when you asked her to marry you?'

'No. I spoke of our friendship, our affection, but I didn't pretend to a love I didn't feel because it would have been dishonest, and that would have insulted her. She'd have seen through every word and despised me as a liar. And it seemed the best way because she was very cheerful, agreed with me about our marriage.'

'Poor Lisetta,' Ruth mused. 'I suppose she concealed her feelings, afraid of frightening you off. She must have thought, when you were married, she could win your love.'

'Yes, I finally realised that,' he groaned. 'I don't know how I could have been so blind.'

'Because she meant you to be. She was fighting for something she wanted, and she knew the way to do it. Good for her.'

He looked at her strangely.

'You're forgetting how badly it ended for her.'

'No, I'm not. The future is always a mystery. You can only take the step you see ahead, and deal with the consequences as they happen. She sounds like a lady with a lot of courage.'

'Courage?'

'Think of the risk she took. How old was she then?'

'About twenty-five.'

'Then she'd waited for you, played high stakes to win the only prize she cared about because nothing less would do. That took real courage.'

In his mind he saw Lisetta again, docile, yielding, eager to please, but sadly without the magic that could have caught his attention. It took an effort to see her through Ruth's eyes, daring, ready to risk everything and smile if she lost.

And she had lost, he thought remorsefully. She'd gained nothing from her marriage but two dead children and the dutiful affection of a man carrying an increasing burden of guilt. But the guilt had been his own fault. She'd never tried to lay that burden on him.

'You're right,' he said suddenly. 'She was a brave woman. I meant to be a good husband, and at first things went well. She became pregnant almost at once, and we were happy. I was grateful to her for giving my father hope, and also on my own account.

'I found that I loved the idea of being a father. That took me by surprise. I'd never thought of it before, but suddenly I wanted it so much, and Lisetta was the woman who was going to give me my heart's desire. Yes, I think I gave her some happiness then. I hope so, anyway.'

The heavy note in his voice made her ask, 'What happened?'

'She lost the child in the sixth month. That would have been bad enough but my father also died. His health had been on a knife edge while he held on to see his grandchild, and the shock of seeing that hope collapse brought on his last heart attack.

'Lisetta was devastated by what she considered her failure. I tried to reassure her but what could I say? She knew I'd married her for my father's sake and my child's, and now they were both dead. That was when I wished I'd told her some polite lies when I proposed. If I'd said then that I loved her, I might have been able to give her some hope when she was in despair. But I was useless—*useless.*'

He dropped his head into his hands.

When Pietro spoke again his voice was husky.

'I did my best to console her, but it was a pretty useless best. She kept saying that she was sorry she'd let me down, and she'd have another child soon. With every word I felt like a monster, a man who'd destroyed a woman who loved him for his own convenience.

'The worst thing was that she was pinning all her hopes on another baby. She didn't know that the doctor had said she mustn't try again. She wasn't strong enough. I delayed telling her because I knew what it would do to her, but in the end I had to.'

'Poor woman,' Ruth murmured.

'Yes, poor woman,' Pietro said bitterly. 'She had nothing then. Whatever I could give her wasn't enough. She turned to her husband for help, and he failed her.'

'How did she cope?'

'She wouldn't accept it. She said she just needed time to regain her strength, and everything would be fine. I didn't argue because at least it left her some hope, but I had no intention of risking her life with another child. She began taking the pill—'

He broke off and made a helpless gesture, full of despair.

'She swore that she was taking it—that there was no danger of— I shouldn't have believed her. I should have taken better care of her.'

'What happened?'

'She came off the pill, and I only found out when she told me she was pregnant again. I can still see her face, how delighted she was, looking at me for approval.

'I tried to make her understand how dangerous it was, but she wouldn't listen to me or the doctor. He begged her not to go through with it. I told her I'd agree to that, but she wouldn't listen to either of us.'

'Of course not,' Ruth murmured.

'Of course not,' he echoed with a bitterness that was aimed at himself. 'She gave me a love I didn't deserve, and all she cared about was pleasing me. All through her pregnancy she grew weaker, but she was actually happy. There was a time when we thought she might have a chance to come through, and the baby. But then she collapsed.

'Our child was born alive, and she held him in her arms just once before she died. I'll never forget the way she looked at me then, with such joy in her eyes, and such triumph. She'd given me a living child, and that was all she cared about, although she knew her own life was slipping away.

'But then our baby died too, only a few hours after his mother. Her sacrifice had been for nothing. When she was in her coffin I kissed her and told her how sorry I was. Then I put him in her arms again, and now they'll lie together always. Now and then I go back to see them, and always I ask for her forgiveness, but it's too late. I'd give anything to reach her, but I never can.

'Now do you understand why I feel little better than a murderer? I took her life—*for nothing*.'

Ruth didn't answer at first. Pietro's agony of self-reproach seemed imprinted on the air. She would literally have done anything to heal this wound, and it was dawning on her that, incredibly, she had the power to bring him out of this nightmare. But every step must be taken with care, using her mysterious understanding of Lisetta that had come with her own confusions. One wrong move—she shivered.

It could be done, but only if the dice were thrown exactly right.

Taking a deep breath and sending up a prayer, she tossed them into the unknown.

CHAPTER TWELVE

'BUT you didn't take her life,' Ruth said softly.

Pietro stared at her, puzzled. 'What did you say?'

'You didn't take her life. She gave it up.'

'There's no difference.'

'There's every difference. You talk about your father's nineteenth-century attitudes, but then you speak as though Lisetta was a helpless little female caught up in the machinations of the men, with no chance to stand up for herself, and *that's* nineteenth century, if you like.'

'I understand what you're saying, but it doesn't change the fact that I married her for my convenience, and my father's—'

'And she married you because she wanted to be your wife more than anything in the world. More than her pride. More than her safety. More, even, than her life.'

'Am I supposed to feel flattered by that? I might if I thought I was worth it, but no man is,' Pietro replied.

'That was for her to decide. You were worth it to her and you should respect her right to make her own decision. You said your father chose her. There must have been other well-born girls he could have picked. Why her? Maybe because she was already in the house, looking after him?'

'Among other things. I told you he had old-fashioned ideas about suitability, and her father was a visconte as well as being a family friend.'

'And this college professor just happened to be there, caring for him? What about her career? Did she put that on hold?' Ruth questioned, hoping she was getting through to him.

'It was the summer vacation. What are you saying?'

'That she guessed the way your father's thoughts were drifting and she made sure his choice lighted on her. She knew you didn't love her, but it didn't matter because anything was better than life without you.'

'You make her sound like a schemer.'

'No, I don't. I make her sound like a woman in love who focussed on the man she wanted because the thought of living without him was unbearable. Millions of women do that every day. Men too. It makes the world go around. That's what I think she did, and good for her! She had a purpose, and she followed it through to the end.'

'How can you be so sure? You didn't know her.'

'I think I'm beginning to, and to admire her. You had the clue all the time in that story about the dice game, how even as a child she'd risk everything on one throw. I saw it in the picture, and it's only now that I fully understand it. That was her nature. She was a risk-taker. You didn't stand a chance.' Ruth smiled. 'You thought you were the one in charge, the one making conditions, but she was ten times the player you were.'

'I don't know—'

'She wasn't a child when you married her, Pietro. She was strong and clear-eyed, and your marriage didn't come about because you controlled or manipulated her. It happened because she was a mature woman who made her own decisions.

'And there's something else, that I found out about recently. I've been reading the history of her family, and there's an inherited weakness in the women. Many of them have died in childbirth, far more than in other families; not so much recently because medical science has improved, but it's there.'

'Impossible. I'd have known.'

'Would you? I'm talking about history, before you were born. And I don't suppose the family spoke of it in case it damaged the girls' marriage prospects. But Lisetta would have known the chance she was taking.'

He turned and stared at her, stunned as the full implications of this dawned on him.

'Can't you understand?' Ruth pleaded. 'She didn't do it your way, *you* did it *her* way. She staked everything on one throw of the dice, and when she lost she didn't complain. And you should respect that. Grieve for her, yes, but don't feel guilty about her, because that insults her.'

'All the time,' he said huskily. 'All the time—she knew—'

'All the time,' Ruth confirmed. 'She wasn't a helpless victim. She was a high roller, who had the guts to go for broke and see it right through. And she had her moment, at the end, when she held her living baby, and you were there. She didn't lose everything.'

'How do you understand so much about her?' he asked slowly.

'Because I have something in common with her, with my different "selves". She had another 'self' too, only you didn't see it because it happened inside her, but it was her real self, the one that made the decisions, and decided in the end that you were worth any sacrifice. Accept that sacrifice, and honour her for it, but don't feel guilty, because it was her doing, not yours.'

Pietro leaned back against the wall, his face strained.

'How can I let myself believe this?' he whispered. 'I want to believe it so much, but do I have any right?'

'Pietro, you have to believe it for her sake. She doesn't want you to spend the rest of your life grieving and punishing yourself. She only ever wanted the best for you. Live your life. Be happy. That's all she cared about.'

He took her hand and held it against his cheek. All the fight and ferocity had gone out of him.

'Thank you,' he said simply. 'I can't see as far as you do, but I trust your vision more than my own. You'll have to show me.'

For a moment she rubbed her cheek against his hand.

'Then I'll give you a piece of sensible advice,' she said. 'Go to bed, either to sleep or to think. They'll both do you good. You'll be happier in the morning.'

'You'll still be here, won't you?' he asked anxiously.

'Yes, I promise not to go away without telling you.'

Still he hesitated, and suddenly she knew that if she followed him into his room tonight, he wouldn't turn her away. With all her heart she longed to do so, but she forced herself to back off.

The time wasn't right. Whatever future they might have could be endangered if she acted carelessly at this crucial moment.

Don't grab for it. Wait for the dice to give it to you.

'Goodnight,' she said.

'Everything changed—the day you came,' he said slowly.

'Yes. But it's too soon to say how. Goodnight.'

This time he went, although his eyes lingered on her until the door closed.

Ruth was torn by indecision. Had she done the right thing, throwing away her chance when it came? But instinct still told her that the time wasn't right.

That night she fell asleep with her fingers crossed.

She got up next morning to find Pietro dressed and ready to leave.

'I'm going to San Michele,' he said. 'I have to see Lisetta. I don't suppose—would you come with me?'

But Ruth shook her head.

'No, this is just you and her.'

He nodded and turned to go, but something made her call him back.

'Pietro—don't ever take another woman to visit her grave, not now or ever in the future.'

'Does that apply, whoever the woman is?' He was watching her.

'Whoever she is, leave her out of sight. Let Lisetta have you all to herself. She's earned it.'

'Will you promise that you'll still be here when I get back?'

'I promise.'

She had no time to brood over him that day. The business of getting rid of Serafina took several hours and was accomplished by a display of firmness on Ruth's part that won her Minna's glowing admiration.

'No wonder the master dressed you in diamonds,' she said.

'Diamonds?'

'Sewn into the front of your costume last night.'

'I thought that was glass,' she said, aghast. 'No wonder everyone was giving me those funny looks.'

Minna roared with laughter and went off to tell Celia in a knowing way that it wouldn't be long now.

Ruth stayed at home all day, so as to be sure that Pietro would find her there whenever he arrived. When the phone rang she answered it quickly. But it was Mario.

They discussed business for a while, but before he hung up he said, 'I've just checked Pietro's emails. There's one from Gino to say he's going to be here tomorrow. I thought he'd want to know.'

'Thanks, Mario, I'll tell him.'

But when will I tell him? she wondered when she'd hung up.

She'd counted on having a little more time, but this changed things, forcing her hand. If Gino was returning tomorrow then she must take action tonight.

This was how the dice had fallen.

Pietro was calm and peaceful when he returned that evening. She didn't ask questions but waited for him to choose his own moment. Only when Minna had finally left them did he meet her eyes.

'Everything was different,' he said simply. 'In the past I've always asked her forgiveness. This time I just thanked her. And it felt right, as it never has before.'

The dice were rolling into place. Double six. Only one more to go.

'What have you done today?' he asked.

'Thought about you, how you were coping.'

'I can manage now, thanks to you. But you won't go yet, will you?' he added quickly.

'I won't go while you want me.'

From outside came the sound of singing. Going to the window, they saw a 'serenade'—a procession of seven gondolas, each one with a singer, hymning the moon. As they approached the Rialto Bridge a number of sad-faced clowns tossed petals down on them.

'They sound so melancholy,' Ruth observed.

'Carnival is nearly over,' Pietro said. 'And that is always sad.'

The procession of boats had paused outside the palazzo, while the leading singer turned to the window where they were standing, and serenaded them in Venetian.

Pietro began to translate.

'Now the time is passing—all is over—shall we meet again another year—or shall we have only our memories?'

He stood just behind her, his hands laid gently on her shoulders.

'I've got something to tell you,' she said. 'Mario checked your email and he says Gino's coming back tomorrow.'

He reacted at once, snatching his hands from her shoulders and stepping back.

'Why do you do that?' she asked, swinging round to him.

'Gino—'

'So what, Gino? He's not part of my life now. I don't love him, I love you. And that's not going to change.'

'It might. When you see him—'

She reached out, putting her hands on either side of his face.

'You're doing it again, trying to take charge of

every detail. But I say how I feel, not you. I make this decision, not you, and I've made it. I'm a grown woman, and I know what I want.'

'And what—do you want?' he asked, almost hypnotised by the force she radiated.

'This,' she said, and drew his head down to hers.

He laid his hands on her, unable to resist that much. But he was still fighting himself, not moving his lips on hers, except to say, 'This is dangerous.'

'Yes, isn't it wonderful?' she challenged him. 'Stop thinking with your head. That's more dangerous than anything.'

She kissed him again, and when she drew back he was smiling.

'It's not supposed to be this way,' he murmured. 'I'm expected to be the one in charge.'

'Unless you meet someone who knows more than you do.'

'Yes, you know so much more than me.'

'I know everything,' she confirmed. 'Come with me. Carnival will soon be over, and we must toss the masks away.'

Ruth took him to her room, where the bed was a little wider than his, although not by much. She was without false modesty. She'd been naked in his arms once before, without knowing it. Now she wanted to relish every moment, so she stripped off her clothes in seconds and stood before him, asking a silent question.

She had her answer when he dropped down to his knees and laid his face against her breasts, enclosing her in his arms. It was a gesture of surrender, an acknowledgement that his love and need of her was stronger than the demons that had haunted him.

She closed her hands behind his head, drawing him closer, inviting him to make his home in her love and care, and his caresses told her that it was where he wanted to be. He too discarded his clothes quickly and they clung together, not hurrying because every moment was precious and they had never dared to think they would reach this moment.

She was smaller than he remembered, more delicate, yet stronger. He understood that strength now. He'd discovered it in her spirit, now he found it in her flesh that was strangely elusive, while at the same time her clasp on him had a power and purpose that thrilled him. When she reached for him he felt enfolded in her love, carried to safety.

An old-fashioned man, he had never before thought of seeking safety in a woman, yet from her he craved it. She could give him love and pleasure, but she could also do what no other woman could do, and strengthen him against the world.

The world seemed very far away at this moment. Their trust in each other was instinctive. When he caressed her he found no hesitancy. She offered herself to him gladly, as though every inch of her body had waited only for him. He loved her for that, but he loved her even more for the look in her eyes as she watched him, a look of delight, expectancy and fulfilment.

He loved her too for her readiness to commit to him while not knowing what the morrow held, for the way she returned caress for caress, wanting him, making him feel like a king.

He cupped one breast in his hand, feeling how naturally it fitted there, as though made just for him, how swiftly the nipple peaked at the touch of his lips, how bravely it spoke of her desire.

She laughed softly and the sound went through him, shredding his control so that it was a struggle not to take her swiftly. But he forced himself to wait, to give her time to flower, even though the sound of her breathing was already telling him what he longed to know.

Ruth lay back, luxuriating in the joy of what was happening. The touch of his fingers, his lips, sent pleasure glowing through her, bringing her closer to the longed-for moment when she could let go of control. But greater than this was the joy of seeing his defences fall away, knowing that he'd abandoned them because his trust in her was complete.

She couldn't see him very well, but well enough to know that he was everything she'd hoped and more; lean, straight, with a power that he kept leashed, but not completely hidden.

They were one in the heart before they were one in the body, and neither of them asked more.

She knew that the protective side of him was so strong that even now his fears for her troubled him, but they were slipping away as his desire for her took control of him, until at last he forgot everything but the urgency of claiming her.

She was ready for him, so that the moment of their union was easy, an inevitable coming together, that made the world stop for the briefest second before starting again with a fierce urgency that didn't let up until they were both exhausted.

Ruth thought she cried out, or the voice might have been his. There were no words, only the triumph of coming home and knowing that it was the right place at last.

Afterwards he propped himself on one elbow to look down on her. His face was suffused with his love but, being Pietro, he had to ask her worriedly, 'Is everything all right with you?'

She smiled. 'Everything's wonderful with me. Stop worrying. It doesn't depend on Gino.'

'How did you know I was thinking of him?'

'Because I know you. You worry about things, all the time. But he can't affect us. I wanted you to know that. Gino can give me some information, but he can't touch me here.' She laid her hand over her heart. 'Don't you believe me?'

'I couldn't bear to lose you—not now.'

'You never will.' She put her arms up around his neck. 'I'm not even going to go away tonight.'

The last throw. A perfect six.

According to Mario, Gino's email had given no indication of when he would arrive.

'Or he may not arrive at all,' Ruth observed next morning. 'He might back out, like last time. I hope not. I want this out of the way and done with.'

'Suppose you don't remember the missing bits?'

'Then I'll manage without them.' She smiled at him. 'If only you knew how unimportant all that seems now.'

'I'd better call Mario and tell him we're not coming in.'

His manner was still troubled, and she knew that only one thing could truly ease his mind. As he turned to the phone she began to get out her books to do some work. But then a sound made her look up.

Gino was standing there, watching her.

How many times in her dreams—nightmares?—had she turned to find him there, looking just as he had once before, as handsome as ever, just as she remembered him?

Now he was here, a fantasy brought to life, for he was unchanged: tall, slim, a slightly hesitant smile on his face. That hesitancy had always been part of his charm. This was Gino, just as she recalled him.

And yet—something was different, something wrong, if only she could pinpoint it. There was no time to analyse it now. Her heart was beating with some emotion she didn't understand. It was too much like fear.

Gino was looking puzzled, and she realised that he'd never seen her looking like this before.

'Ruth? It is Ruth, isn't it?'

'Yes, it's me. Hallo, Gino.'

She had the sensation that her mind had split into several sections, each one working at full stretch, noticing something different. Gino stared as if he couldn't believe his eyes. Behind him was a young woman who might have been pretty if her make-up hadn't been too lavish and her dress too tight. Above all Ruth was aware of Pietro, holding himself still and tense, watching them.

'I want you to meet someone,' Gino said with an awkward laugh. 'This is Josie, my fiancée.'

He emphasised the last word, very slightly, and drew the girl forward, positioning her just in front of him, almost as though he wanted her to protect him. And that, of course, was exactly what he did want, Ruth thought.

She could almost have laughed aloud. For a while she had adored this man, thought the sun rose and set on him. Now he was afraid of her.

And in that moment she identified the subtle difference that had troubled her from the start. Gino looked shifty. The shiftiness was there in his eyes, in his smile. It was there in the fact that he could only face her with another woman to stand between him and trouble. It had probably always been there, had she not been too infatuated to notice it.

Behind the façade of the shining knight, he was a coward.

It was the word 'coward' that did it. Suddenly the world grew dark, shuddering around her.

'Oh God!' she screamed. 'No, no, *no*!'

Dimly she could sense Pietro's alarm, his look of horror as he rose and came to her. But his face faded, replaced by Gino, not as he was now, but as he'd been that night, handsome, shining, full of adoration for her before the world had fallen in on them.

'No,' she cried. 'I don't believe it—it can't be true—'

Gino didn't say a word. He only looked at her uneasily as his worst fears were realised.

'You—' she gasped '—you—*you ran away and left me*.'

She was back in the car park, and suddenly all the things that had been obscure were horribly clear. The thugs knocked her to the ground, kicking her. She screamed to Gino but he was running away as fast as he could. At the last moment he looked behind him, his face full of terror, then ran on faster than ever, abandoning her to her attackers. Then she passed out.

'You left me to their mercy,' she repeated slowly.

'Ruth, what is it?' Pietro was there, holding her, providing the one sure point in a disintegrating world, the way he always had.

'When we were attacked in the cark park, he just ran away.'

'That's not true,' Gino began to bluster. 'I went to get help—you told me to—'

'No, you saved your own skin,' she said, staring at him as though seeing him for the first time, which, in a sense, she was.

'You don't know what happened—you don't remember—'

'I do now. It's coming back. I could have died because you abandoned me. *Get away from me.*'

She cried out the last words because Gino had

made a protesting gesture towards her. But Pietro was there, warding him off.

'Stay away,' he said firmly.

'Look, it wasn't as bad as she says—'

'Yes, it was,' Ruth choked. 'I'm surprised you came to the hospital to see me even once—'

'I-I had to find out how you were—' he stammered.

'No, you wanted to find out if I was safely dead, so that I couldn't give you away. When I couldn't remember anything you must have thought luck was with you. That's why you dashed back to Italy so fast.'

'I did what was best for you,' Gino tried to plead. 'It just upset you to see me around, so I left—for your sake.'

'You lying, cheating jerk.' The words burst from the girl at his side. 'You told me she'd broken your heart.'

'No wonder you've kept away this year,' Pietro snapped. 'You were afraid I'd find out what a worm you are, and fire you. And you were right to be afraid. The sooner you're out of this place, the better. Get out and don't let me see you again. Ever.'

'Oh, now look—be reasonable—'

'Reasonable?' Pietro echoed savagely. 'You think—'

'No, Pietro, stop.' Ruth laid a hand on his arm. 'Forget it. Let it go.'

'Let it go? After what he did to you?'

But the clouds that had descended on her so fast were retreating just as quickly in the face of the truth. She could stand up and speak strongly, still holding on to Pietro, but now as much to reassure him as to claim his support.

'But it doesn't matter, don't you see?' she said. '*He* doesn't matter. It's over. Finished. We've found out what we wanted to know, and we can take it from there.'

'Are you quite sure?' he asked, searching her face.

'I was never more sure of anything in my life. I love you, and only you. Is everything all right now?'

'Yes,' he said quietly. 'If it's all right with you, then everything's all right with me.'

He drew her close in a fervent embrace, and when they looked up again they were alone.

'He's gone,' Pietro said.

'So let him go.'

From somewhere deep in the building Josie's voice floated back, 'Just push off!'

And Gino's answering, 'If you'd just listen to me—*ow*! What did you do that for?'

'What do you think?'

They faded to nothing.

'I think she's got his measure,' Pietro observed.

'Can you stop worrying now?' Ruth asked tenderly.

He shook his head in wry self-understanding. 'No, I've just got a new set of things to worry about. What will I do if you leave me, if you don't love me, if you won't marry me—?'

'I can set your mind at rest about that one right now.'

'Then I'll find another one. Suppose I disappoint you, drive you away with my awkward behaviour—' He checked, answered by her fond smile.

'Just promise to be here always,' he said. 'Love me to the end, and I won't ask anything else.'

'There isn't anything else,' she said. 'Nothing else in all the world.' She touched his face. 'I'll have to teach you that.'

'Teach me anything you like, as long as you're here.'

'As long as for ever,' she said.

Carnival ended with fireworks set off from boats far out in the lagoon, while an orchestra played on land. It began at eleven o'clock and finished on the stroke of midnight, for that was the start of Lent, the time of repentance.

'Not for me,' Pietro said as they wandered back home, his arm about her. 'No repentance, no regrets—ever.'

'You can't be sure of that,' she reminded him.

He regarded her fondly. 'Yes, I can.'

Now it was over. The crowds wended their way back to hotels and the next day most of them would be gone. Already Venice seemed to be growing quieter as they opened the side door of the palazzo, and found Toni waiting there with an expectant look.

'I was planning to go to bed,' Pietro informed the awkward hound.

Toni looked at him.

'He's entitled to his walk,' Ruth insisted. 'We couldn't take him out before because of the fireworks.'

'Come on, then.'

They went towards the Rialto Bridge, and stood there a moment, watching as a convoy of gondolas approached, on their way home. As they neared the bridge the lead gondolier called out, congratulating them on their coming marriage.

'How does he know?' Ruth asked.

'He's Minna's nephew. And the one behind him is Minna's godson and the one behind him—well, you get the picture.'

'You mean all Venice knows?'

'Certain to.'

Toni put his paws on the stone balustrade and wuffed, and the gondoliers hailed him too, before gliding on under the bridge, and home.

'The whole of Venice is planning our wedding,' he said. 'And the rest of our lives probably, how we're going to open up the palazzo and return it to its glory days.'

'Do we have to?' she asked quickly. 'Cinderella isn't used to living a grand life.'

'I'm afraid the Contessa Bagnelli will have to put up with a bit of grandeur, some of the time.'

'I suppose so,' she sighed. 'It's just that I love those little rooms. They're like a nest. I'd like to stay right there, but I suppose that's unrealistic of me.'

'We could still keep it. When you get mad at me, you can take refuge in the nest. Just leave me a note saying that you never want to see me again, and I'll know where to bring the red roses.'

They laughed in fond understanding.

'In any case,' she mused as they left the Rialto and strolled on under a narrow archway and over a tiny bridge, 'the nest is very tiny. It won't be big enough for three of us—or four—'

He stopped abruptly. *'No,'* he said.

'I thought you wanted children.'

'Not like—I mean, it's up to you. I'll never pressure you, or even ask you.'

For a moment his voice was tense as his ghosts walked again and she hastened to ease his mind.

'You won't have to ask,' she promised. 'It'll just happen. Stop worrying.' She put her hands on either side of his head and repeated, 'Stop worrying. I'm here, and I'm going to take care of everything.'

He gave a self-mocking smile. 'You don't know how good that sounds.'

'From now on you'll have me to look after you.'

'Then I have nothing else to worry about—' his face clouded again '—as long as all is well with you. I saw you when you were waiting for Gino, and you were afraid, I could tell. Suppose you did love him, after we—?'

'No, it wasn't like that,' she assured him. 'I was only afraid of what I might remember, that maybe I'd done something stupid, something that would cast a blight over you and me, or even send my mind back into the shadows. That was the only fear.'

'And instead, Gino turns out to be a cowardly little swine whom no woman should look at twice,' Pietro said with a touch of anger.

'Hush, it doesn't matter.'

'How can you say that what he did to you doesn't matter?'

'All right, it matters, but only because it sent me to you. If he'd behaved well I might have married him, and then you and I would have met too late.'

He nodded. 'That's a terrifying thought, because I couldn't have met you without loving you, and if it was too late—'

He tightened his arm about her.

'That would have been truly a life lived in the shadows,' he said. 'With nothing but pain and regret.'

'Do you remember the first night we met?' she asked. 'We talked then about shadows, about how they never ended.'

'I remember.'

'But they have ended now. Gino has gone from my mind as thoroughly as he's gone from my heart. Now there's only you, always.'

Pietro replied, not in words, but with a kiss that was long and gentle.

They walked on for a while, listening to the night. Venice was quiet except for the distant sound of laughter, the fading music that meant the gondoliers were going home, the soft cry of seagulls.

'Contessa Bagnelli,' she mused, trying the name for size. 'I just can't quite see myself living up to all the pomp. Life in a London suburb doesn't exactly fit you for it.'

'But you'll do it wonderfully, with the help of your friends—all seventy thousand of them.'

She understood at once. The people who lived here all the time, the true Venetians who stood out from all other people in the world by their courage, their readiness to face any trouble, and, above all, their generosity.

Her very first day here they had kept protective eyes on her as she blundered around, then guided Pietro to her rescue. Her friends were there again now, opening windows overhead, looking down at the two of them, smiling with delight, whispering their good wishes, welcoming her into the family.

'*Buona notte,* signore.'

'*Buona notte, Alfredo, Renato, Maria…*' He knew all their names.

From all sides the words floated down around them. 'Is it true? Please say that it's true—we will be so glad.'

He laughed up at them. 'Wait and see,' he teased.

But they had already seen what they cared about. Their friend was laughing again. All was well.

'You're one of us already,' Pietro told her. 'And we'll never let you go.'

Overhead, a hundred eyes watched them drifting contentedly on their way, with Toni padding softly behind them, until the friendly darkness swallowed them up.

0608/05b

On sale
4th July 2008

Don't miss out on these fabulous stories!

The Tycoon's Mistress

by Carole Mortimer

Featuring

His Cinderella Mistress
The Unwilling Mistress
The Deserving Mistress

Available at WHSmith, Tesco, ASDA, and all good bookshops
www.millsandboon.co.uk